TRUE LOVE TO THE RESCUE

I put my arms around Sally's waist and lifted her off the ground. As I did this, Tommy let out a yell, "Kidnapping . . . Kidnapping . . . Kidnapping," as he pointed to me holding Sally.

Then he ran down the aisle, took a right turn into one of the side corridors and disappeared through a mall exit.

The commotion was something to see. As the Savior's goons and the two cops rushed up to us, Sally and I put our lips together in an Oscar-winning kiss. And held it.

"What the hell is going on here?" asked one of the cops.

I put Sally down. Slowly. We both smiled.

"He just popped the question," Sally told the cop.

"What question?"

"Oh . . . you know . . . silly goose . . . would I marry him," replied Sally.

"What was the yelling about?"

"Oh, that was Ralph . . . he's very emotional . . . he thinks Granny stole me from him . . . he's really a dear, and he'll get over it."

Other Avon Flare Books by
M. Arthur Bogen

DOUBLE DEALING
BARELY UNDERCOVER

MIND GAMES

A BURCHARDT & DECKER MYSTERY

M. ARTHUR BOGEN

AN AVON  FLARE BOOK

MIND GAMES is an original publication of Avon Books.
This work has never before appeared in book form.

AVON BOOKS
A division of
The Hearst Corporation
1790 Broadway
New York, New York 10019

First Flare Printing, March 1984

FLARE TRADEMARK REG. U. S. PAT. OFF. AND IN
OTHER COUNTRIES, MARCA REGISTRADA, HECHO EN
U. S. A.

Printed in the U. S. A.

WFH 10 9 8 7 6 5 4 3 2 1

MIND GAMES

CHAPTER 1

I felt like they had washed my brain and hung it out to dry. And it was getting all shriveled up in the stinking heat, so that I could hardly use it. The room stank because twenty kids were jammed into it and none of them had washed for two days. I can't remember if I had had any sleep during those forty-eight hours.

A series of loud speakers played music at an ear-shattering volume. When the music stopped, the lectures started. The preachers took turns telling us that the "Prophet" loved us and would soon reveal the secrets of a perfect life. We would receive this glorious revelation only if our souls were "worthy." How could I know if I was "worthy" if I could barely remember who I was?

To save my sanity and to keep some control over my mind and body, I concentrated on recalling my life. A life that seemed to come to an end the day before yesterday.

My name was (and may still be) Grant Decker. I'm eighteen years old, just graduated from high school where my six feet one height and my one hundred and eighty pounds enabled me to win a varsity letter on the football team. My hair is blond like my mother's. Not dark like Sally's.

Sally! Oh, God! The instant that I thought of Sally, I felt a cold fear, an almost hysterical panic, radiate from my stomach. We had come to this place together. But they had separated us and I had not seen her for two days. To calm the fear, I focused on thoughts of Sally.

Sitting cross-legged on the bare wooden floor, I closed my eyes and could see her five feet nine, exquisitely proportioned figure dressed in denim shorts, close-fitting T-shirt and leather sandals. Her crystal blue eyes looked at the world with warmth, humor and amused tolerance. She was also eighteen and had been in my high-school graduating class. We had known each other for two years.

The vision of Sally was blown out of my mind by a shout from the front of the room: "He LOVES you, brother!"

The voice drilled through my brain like a pellet shot from a high-powered air gun.

If he loves me so much, why doesn't he let me get some brotherly sleep? Doesn't the Bible say that we are our brother's sleeper? Damn . . . I'm freaking out.

And to think that it all started because we wanted to help a friend.

Right now, Sally and I are trapped in a four-bedroom farmhouse in southern California, not far from San Diego. The house is located on a hill about a mile from the highway along a narrow dirt road. The permanent residents are a group of about twenty perpetually smiling young people and four older leaders. None of whom can utter a sentence that doesn't include the word *love*. I'm being bombarded with "We love you" . . . "The Prophet loves you" . . . "The Lord loves you" . . . "Your parents *don't* love you."

Always with a smile.

The first time they told me that my parents didn't love me, I felt that the best response would be to punch their teeth in so that it would be difficult to keep smiling. But, weird as it sounds, I'm beginning to believe them.

They call themselves "Children of the Savior." And devote themselves to rescuing souls from the evil, corrupt world. The world I used to live in.

Sally and I came here on the "Savior's Chariot." An old, beat-up, creaking school bus owned by the "Children of the Savior." We came of our own free will. Not to join the group but to look for a friend of ours: Janice Gleason, who disappeared about three months ago.

Janice was a close friend of Sally's. Which may have struck some people as odd. Sally is tall, athletic and beautiful with a spontaneous, outgoing personality. Janice is small, thin, mousy-looking and somewhat introverted. But she is intelligent and always willing to help others.

A few times Sally and Janice worked together on school projects or assignments. Sally told me that after finishing their work, they'd talk far into the night about life.

During the Easter vacation, Janice went to visit her aunt and uncle in southern California. A few days after her arrival in California, she telephoned her parents and told them that she had met some wonderful people and would be spending some time with them. Before her mother could question her about who the people were, Janice said good-bye and hung up the phone.

When Mrs. Gleason called her sister to find out what was happening, her sister told her not to worry because Janice was involved in "spiritual work." She was vague about where the work was being done and who was involved.

The Easter recess ended but Janice didn't return home.

The Gleasons received two more telephone calls from Janice. She gave her parents a box number and post-office address that could be used to write to her. During the second and last call, Mrs. Gleason ordered Janice to come home, and received a strange response: "I'm eighteen years old and you are not my parents," she said, and hung up.

The Gleasons were frantic and tried to get help

from the California authorities but got bogged down in legal technicalities.

Sally offered to help by writing to Janice to persuade her to come home. She received no reply to three letters.

A few days after our graduation from high school, I was with Sally in her home when she received a telephone call from Janice.

"Hello, is this Sally?"

"Yes."

"This is Grace."

"Who?"

"Grace . . . you knew me as Janice."

"Janice!"

Sally pointed to the kitchen and indicated that I should pick up the extension phone. I did.

"Oh, I'm so happy you called. I miss you. Did you get my letters?" Sally asked.

"Yes."

"Why didn't you answer them?"

"There is no time for personal indulgence."

Janice's voice was flat and drained of feeling. Sally sensed that she must tread carefully in talking to Janice, or their conversation would end abruptly.

"Oh, I understand," said Sally.

"No you don't . . . no outsider understands."

"I'm really trying to . . ."

"I'm calling you to ask a favor."

"What is it?"

"Please tell those people who call themselves my parents to leave me alone and stop what they are doing to interfere with my life. They have no right."

"I'll tell them."

"Thank you."

"What are you doing now?" asked Sally.

"The work of the Savior."

"Sounds worthwhile . . . how long are you planning on doing this work?"

"The rest of my life."

10

"Oh."

"There is no higher calling."

"I understand . . . are there others with you?"

"Yes . . . many . . . and we are increasing . . . we are called the 'Children of the Savior.' "

"Where are you?"

"That's not important."

"I miss you, Janice."

"Grace."

"Yes . . . Grace."

Sally was becoming frustrated and upset. She couldn't penetrate the shell that seemed to surround Janice. It was as if a new and unfamiliar personality had taken over Janice's mind. In desperation, Sally asked, "Are there any boys there?"

"Certainly. The Savior welcomes men and women."

"Anyone in particular?"

"No."

"Oh."

"I'm to be married during the autumnal equinox."

"That's wonderful! Who is he?"

"I don't know."

Sally looked at the phone as if it were transmitting a foreign language. When she recovered she said, "Janice . . . Grace, did you say that you were getting married?"

"Yes."

". . . and that you don't know who you're marrying?"

"Yes . . . the Savior will tell me . . . when the time is right."

"You mean, the Savior chose a husband for you and you have no say in it?"

"That's not important."

"Since when?"

"You're becoming hostile . . . but I forgive you."

"Forgive me? . . . I . . . I . . ."

After a few seconds, Sally gained control of her emotions and said, "I'm happy for you."

There was some mumbling in the background on Janice's end of the line, then Janice said, "I have to go now. Remember, tell those people to stop meddling in my life."

With that she hung up.

When I joined Sally in the living room, she was staring at the phone and slowly shaking her head in disbelief.

"This isn't possible . . . I've heard of it but never believed it."

We reported the conversation to Janice's parents. They were shattered and totally at a loss as to what they could or should do.

Sally and I had planned a backpacking trip in California and were flying to San Diego in a few days to start our walking tour. It seemed natural that we should try to find Janice and determine exactly what had happened to her. I didn't say it but I thought that it was just possible that Janice had found the answer to life's craziness.

We promised to report to the Gleasons as soon as we had any information.

When we landed in San Diego, we asked around and soon found out that groups of kids hung out at nearby beaches. Somebody thought that they had seen a sign on a bus that read "Children of the Savior." He recalled the location as being Mission Beach.

We picked up our backpacks and boarded a bus that would take us to Mission Beach. As we settled in our seats, Sally said, "I have the uncomfortable feeling that we are about to poke our noses into a place with no welcome mat."

"Just a harmless poke by a pair of friendly noses," I assured her.

"From what I have read and heard, these cults are as happy to see nosy outsiders as a flock of lambs is to see a hungry lion."

"The Bible tells us that the lion and the lamb shall lie down together."

12

"That's true . . . but the lamb will get very little sleep."

I thought about this for a while and realized that we might have a problem if we started asking prying questions.

"I think that the best approach is to pretend that we want to join the group," I suggested.

Sally agreed.

As we were walking across the parking lot at Mission Beach, we spotted it. It was a big, old, yellow bus with a banner hung along one side reading "The Savior's Chariot." Nearby were two young men and a young woman surrounding and earnestly talking to a girl dressed in a black bikini and short, orange, terry-cloth robe. The strangest part of the scene was that the men were wearing shirts, ties and jackets. And this was June in a beach parking lot! The three saviors must have had major smile-graft surgery because they never relaxed their inane grins.

I heard one of them say to the surrounded girl, "Suzy, we can see that you have a beautiful soul and you deserve a life of peace and happiness."

Suzy looked confused and she replied, "My life is not too bad."

"But are you *really* happy?"

"I . . . I don't know."

"See? . . . You're not happy . . . you need to be understood and loved."

His sales pitch was getting into high gear and his eyes glazed over as he overdosed on love and understanding.

The other neatly dressed young man said, "My name is Rick and I'd like you to come to dinner with us and meet the rest of the family. After you meet the family, we'll bring you back. It will be a lovely experience."

Suzy wavered, then said, "I'm not dressed. I only have my bathing suit and robe."

"Don't worry. One of the beautiful sisters will lend you a dress."

Suzy gave a doubtful nod.

The young man took her arm and said, "Come. Let me get you a cool glass of orange juice and I'll find you a comfortable seat on the bus."

With that, he led her to the bus.

Sally looked at me and gave me a quick wink. She then approached the remaining young man and said in her sweetest voice, "Pardon me, sir. Could you tell us where we could find an inexpensive restaurant?"

The young man's smile widened another two inches, "Of course, dear. Are you hungry?"

Which is kind of a funny question to ask somebody looking for a restaurant. I was tempted to reply that we were itinerent food critics and were two restaurants behind on our current assignment.

Sally smiled to show her appreciation of his keen intelligence. "Yes. We are a little short of funds and can't afford an expensive meal."

The fellow did the impossible. He added another inch to his smile. He looked like a fisherman who had just sunk his hook into a world-class sailfish.

"My name is Paul. What is your name?"

"Sally."

"That's a beautiful name."

Turning to me, he asked, "And your name?"

"Grant."

I wondered if he was going to notice how beautiful my name was. He didn't.

"That's a strong name," he declared. Turning to Sally, he said, "There's no need to spend your money in a restaurant. Have dinner with the family and meet some beautiful people."

"That's very beautiful of you," observed Sally.

"Is that the family bus?" I asked, pointing to the yellow school bus.

"Yes."

"We've heard some lovely things about you beautiful people from a friend of ours, Janice Gleason. Do you know her?"

His face went blank. The smile faded for a moment. But he quickly recovered and put on a three-quarter smile.

"That must be her name from her previous life. The Savior provides us with new names when we do his work."

I looked at Sally. There seemed to be no alternative. Paul was not about to offer any help in finding Janice. We'd have to go to the family estate and try to find her ourselves.

We agreed to have dinner with Paul and his beautiful family. Only it turned out to be a lot more than dinner.

When Rick, Paul and the neatly dressed girl had loaded about twelve dinner guests on the bus, they cranked up the chariot and headed out of the parking lot. I looked around at our fellow passengers. They were all young. I saw Suzy in her black bikini and terry robe. She seemed slightly dazed. As though she wasn't quite sure why she had agreed to go.

About an hour later, we turned off the highway and drove onto a dirt road. Soon we were pulling into a parking area where a number of cars were parked. Much later I found out that the cars were "contributed" by the new recruits to the cause of the founder and the leader of the "Children of the Savior." The cars were sold and the money turned over to the leader.

As the bus was being parked, a number of people came out of the large frame house. They met us as we descended from the bus. They hugged us and said, "We love you, brother. We love you, sister."

Everybody was smiling. They must have all graduated with honors from the Institute of Perpetual Smiles.

They took the girls into one part of the house and the fellows into another area. Sally and I became separated. At the time, I didn't give this too much thought.

They sat us down on the floor. An older man came into the room, looked us over and announced, "Welcome to our home. I'm Jeremiah. Please call me Jerry. I'm here to answer all your questions. But before that and before we have dinner, Brother Joshua will honor us with some songs. To put us in a happy frame of mind."

Brother Joshua came in carrying an electric guitar, which he plugged into a set of loudspeakers. Ole Josh was a tall skinny kid with a bad complexion and a faraway look in his eyes. He played "You Are My Sunshine" at a volume seven decibels higher than music played in a disco. It numbed my mind. We were invited to sing along. At first I resisted but I soon found that I was the only one not singing. Not to be conspicuous, I joined in. Joshua played on and we sang for about an hour. Popular songs, inspirational songs and gospel tunes. After a while, I forgot where I was.

The dinner was served buffet-style. We were given paper plates, and helped ourselves. The meal consisted of frankfurters, french fried potatoes, packaged cakes and Coca-Cola. All we wanted.

When we had finished, Jeremiah-Call-Me-Jerry addressed us.

"I'm so happy to be here with you and to tell you about the beautiful life, the loving life, the perfect life. The life we live for our leader. The life with meaning. Not the selfish, mean, evil life outside. We give thanks to the miracle that has shown us the way." Etc. Etc.

He lectured about an hour on the terrible sins of the world and the need for goodness and light to shine from our souls and to illuminate the way to salvation. After a while, I could only hear his voice and not the words.

When Jeremiah finished, Joshua plugged in his

guitar and drove the music into our bodies through our ears, up our noses and through our skins. It was paralyzing.

Then another lecturer took over. He was even more upset about the condition of the world than Call-Me-Jerry. And louder. Then Josh took a few more whacks at us with his screaming guitar. Jerry materialized again and reminded us how much he loved us and how lucky we were to be offered a new life.

It must have been about two o'clock in the morning when all the noise stopped and everybody collapsed into sleep. Stretched out on the floor.

Three hours later, I heard a guitar twanging "You Are My Sunshine." I couldn't believe it. It seemed like I had just closed my eyes. Then a voice called out, "Sing along, brothers and sisters. The Lord has given us a new day of joy and happiness."

A rising volume of voices began to sing. I tried to cover my ears to get some more sleep. A hand was laid on my shoulder and a sweet female voice said, "Awake, beautiful brother. The dawn is about to release the sun to shine on our love."

Love at five o'clock in the morning! Only owls and insomniacs would dare to open their eyes at that hour. Cautiously, I opened one eye and saw a pretty girl with long blond hair kneeling over me. Of course, she was smiling.

"We are so happy that you are going to share this sunrise with us," she declared.

Insanely, I smiled back. Then sat up.

"We will go outside and up the mountain to watch the beauty of the world come alive; then we will have breakfast," she said.

"Can I go to the bathroom and wash up first?" I asked.

"Of course, brother. The bathroom is over there."

I looked to where she was pointing. There was a

line of about ten guys waiting to get in. I looked back at her.

"Is there another bathroom?"

"Not yet. The Savior will soon provide more."

I wanted to tell her that it might be better to rely on a good building contractor to do the providing but she seemed so sweet and sincere that I didn't want to hurt her feelings. She left me.

By the time I got into the bathroom, it was filled with dirty paper towels and it stank. I hoped that a dozen Air Wicks were on the heavenly shopping list.

As I was leaving the bathroom, the pretty girl with the long blond hair took my arm, smiled and announced, "The dawn is waiting for us. Let us go out and give praise that we have found each other and will soon reside in peace and happiness."

It was as if she had memorized that speech and gave it on cue. But it sounded good to me anyway.

They hustled us out of the house into the predawn light. I could see the young men who had come in the bus with us yesterday. But none of the young women. Each new fellow was being attended by a "family" member. Usually a smiling girl. They trotted us up a short distance to the crest of the hill above the house. We all sat down facing east. And waited for the sun to announce the miracle of a new day. It seems that the sun would not rise unless we sang. So to make sure that there was no slipup in the sunrise, Joshua led us in singing inspiring tunes.

To be honest, when the golden shafts of the rising sun appeared over the distant horizon, it was truly beautiful. I felt a sense of awe.

When the sun was fully over the horizon, we went back to the house for breakfast. They served us milk and cereals. Sugar Krisps, Froot Loops, Candied Krunchies, etc. And fruit drinks. Kool-Aid, fruit punch and orangeade. It was filling.

Then the music started and only stopped when a speaker got up to tell us about the new life of joy, happiness and peace that we were about to enter. Soon I began to think that it sounded like a wonderful idea. No hassles. No decisions. Surrounded by beautiful people who only wanted to give . . . not take. All working together to bring the world to universal love. It was grand, noble and satisfying. I had found the answer to life's problems.

Near the end of the day, thoughts of Sally began to float through my head. I wanted to tell her about the marvelous thing that was happening to me. As soon as I began to look around, the girl with the long blond hair, whose name was Faith, asked me, "Is there something you want, beautiful brother?"

"Yes. Where is Sally?"

"Who?"

"Sally. The girl I came with."

"Oh. She will be with us."

"Yes. But where is she now?"

"She is with the sisters."

"Where?"

"Don't worry, brother, the Savior is watching her."

Faith smiled compassionately and touched my arm.

Something seemed wrong but I couldn't concentrate because I was being urged to join in the singing. I sang and forgot about Sally.

The songs and inspirational speeches continued until long after midnight. Interrupted only by the evening meal consisting of some kind of soup, bread and a stew containing frankfurters. My mind was totally numb but I felt euphoric.

When they finally let us lie down to get some sleep, I stretched out on the floor. Just before I slipped into a formless dream, a cold fear drifted through my mind.

The fright was so intense that I felt I had to shrink

into invisibility in order to hide from my thoughts. I knew that I had to get away quickly or I would be lost forever.

But I didn't know how to escape.

CHAPTER 2

I don't remember waking up but I found myself surrounded by smiling kids greeting another dawn. Their eyes were glazed. Probably from lack of sleep, too much junk food and constant assaults on their minds with music and speeches. And no silence in which to assemble any coherent thoughts. Their brains, and mine, must be turning into mush. We were being conditioned.

The surprise was that, for a few minutes at least, my brain tried to function independently. It was thinking thoughts of doubt and fear, not faith and love. But only for fleeting moments. It was easy to surrender to the comfort of obeying and not thinking. To loving and being accepted.

I knew that I had to fight to keep control of my own identity and resist being hammered into a mindless organism. I must block out the sights and sounds around me and concentrate on something outside of myself. But what? Then I knew: Sally!

To hide what was going on in my head, I froze my face into a sappy smile and kept nodding my head like one of those dolls I've seen bobbing in the rear window of an automobile. Not hearing anything or seeing anything.

I willed Sally's image to come to my mind. I could see her crystal blue eyes, the soft fullness of her lips, the delightful curve at the base of her neck as it turned to meet the sweet roundness of her shoulder. But best of all, if I concentrated hard enough, I could hear the joy of her laughter. As soon as I heard that, I knew that I could get free. A plan formed in my mind.

During the afternoon meal, I spoke to Faith, my ever-present guardian. "Beautiful sister, I never felt real happiness until now."

Faith smiled as though I were St. Peter and had just waved her through the pearly gates into heaven and told her that she was booked to sing a solo with the heavenly choir.

"I am happy for you, brother," she replied.

"I would like to devote my life to working for the 'Children of the Savior.'"

"Bless you."

"But one thing troubles me."

"What is that?"

"I left some worldly possessions behind. In my other life."

"It is not important."

"That is so true. But I would like to give them to the Savior to help us in our work."

Faith's eyes lit up like the lights on a pinball machine when someone scores eight million points. Evidently, being greedy for the cause was a virtue greatly encouraged.

"What is it that you want to contribute, brother?" she asked.

"My car. It's worth four or five thousand dollars. And it's all paid for."

Bingo! She smiled beyond the call of duty. I had touched her lovely soul in its innermost recess.

"That is so generous."

"Just an expression of my love. And besides, I no longer have any use for it."

"I must tell Jeremiah. He will be happy for you."

I suspected that he would be even happier for himself. Faith looked around and saw Jeremiah talking to a group at the other end of the room.

"Wait for me here, brother, while I tell the good news to Jerry."

She strode off to bring the merry tidings to the head honcho.

There was only one minor problem. I had no car.

I watched Faith talking to Jerry. Even from across the room, I could see that the thought of my worldly sacrifice was bringing new joy to the already joy-filled life of Jeremiah. He excused himself from the group he was enlightening and hurried over to where I was standing. Followed by the faithful Faith.

"I have just heard of your inspired and inspiring intention," he exclaimed.

Hanging my head in modesty, I replied, "It's the least I can do."

"Yes. And it will be like freeing yourself from a weight tied around your neck and pulling you down in the sea of worldly possessions and drowning your soul."

I noticed that he wasn't worried about having it tied around his neck and drowning his soul. I guess his soul has inflatable, heavenly water wings.

"Where is your car, brother?" he asked, getting down to business.

"In San Diego."

"Excellent. If you will give us the keys and the title, we shall take care of it for you."

"That is generous of you. But I don't want to put you to all that trouble. I can get it myself."

"No trouble. There is no need to disturb the tranquility that you are finding here."

"That's not the problem."

"What is, then, brother?"

"I left the car in care of my aunt. She has the keys and papers."

"Oh. That's easily solved. We'll write a note that you can sign telling her of your desire."

"That's a wonderful idea. And it would be perfect with anybody but my aunt."

"What do you mean?"

"I know I shouldn't say this about the beloved sister of my dear mother, but she is a suspicious and untrusting woman. She lacks faith and shows an uncommon meanness where money or possessions are concerned. I remember that she once locked Uncle Phil, her husband, out of their house for a week for trying to hide his income tax refund."

Jeremiah didn't look totally convinced but he didn't have much choice.

I continued, "Aunt Phil will only give the keys and the car to me personally."

"I thought Phil was your uncle."

"He is."

"But you just said your *Aunt* Phil."

My brain was tired and had lost track of the cast of characters in my story. It came to attention quickly. I smiled. "Of course. Her name is Phil also."

"Oh."

"Yes. Philip and Phyllis. In the family we call them the two Phils." I almost added "from Philly." Instead, I hurried on and said, "If you get me a ride to San Diego, I'll pick up the car and be back before sunset."

"Yes, of course." He looked at Faith and said, "Get brother Tobias and bring him here."

Faith disappeared. She was back in a few minutes followed by a guy as tall as I am. Weighing twenty pounds more. With a bad complexion.

Jeremiah introduced us, then said to Tobias, "Take the Buick and drive Brother Grant to San Diego to pick up and return with his car."

Tobias nodded.

Jeremiah added, "Brother Grant is your responsibility. See that he is protected by your love and not contaminated by the evils outside."

It sounded like Jeremiah was not fully convinced that I had seen and been dazzled by the light.

Driving back to San Diego, I had another problem to solve. How to get away from Tobias. He kept

24

prattling about how wonderful life with the "family" was and how happy he was that I was now a member. He seemed to be talking in memorized sentences. I couldn't get him to talk about his life before he joined the cult.

As we were passing a shopping mall on the outskirts of San Diego, I pointed and said, "Stop here, brother. I have to make a call to find out if my aunt is home and to tell her that we are coming."

He hesitated for a second, then pulled into the mall parking lot. After he parked the car, I stepped out. So did Tobias. I could see that he was not going to be easy to shake. We headed toward an outdoor telephone booth. A telephone directory was hanging from a chain. I picked up the book, thumbed through some pages and ran my finger down a page, stopped at some name, looked closely, then grunted. Inserting a dime in the phone slot, I dialed seven numbers at random, waited a few seconds, then said, "Hi, Aunt Phil. This is Grant. . . . I'm fine."

A voice at the other end of the phone said, "You have the wrong number."

"Listen, Aunt Phil, I need my car."

"I said you have the wrong number," insisted the voice.

"I can't tell you now, but something wonderful happened to me."

"What's so wonderful about becoming deaf?"

"I'll be there soon."

"If you come, I'll drop a net over you," promised the voice.

"Say hello to Uncle Phil."

"He was just run over by a truck."

"That's wonderful," I said. And hung up.

Tobias had been listening to my end of the conversation.

"Everything is O.K.," I assured him.

We walked back to the car. Tobias slipped in behind the steering wheel. Just as I was about to get into the car, I put my hand over my stomach and said, "I have to go to the bathroom. I'll be right back."

Without waiting for a response, I turned and walked rapidly toward the mall entrance. Tobias must have hesitated before deciding to follow me. I caught a glimpse of him getting out of the car as I ducked through the door. I ran into a department store and rode up to the third floor on an escalator. After wandering around the store for an hour, I left through a different entrance than the one through which I had entered.

Half of my problem was solved. I was free from that gaggle of mind-benders. But the other half was going to be much harder to pull off.

I had to get Sally out.

CHAPTER 3

I had no idea how I was going to do it. In my confused state of mind, I had visions of leaping onto a white stallion, galloping into the cult's camp while waving a six shooter à la John Wayne, scooping up Sally and riding in tandem out of the compound yelling "Yippy Aiy Oh." I wasn't sure but I had the feeling that this plan had one or two minor flaws. Such as the horse-rental agency not accepting MasterCard.

Obviously, the first thing I had to do was to get some rest so that I could start thinking rationally. This I did at a local YMCA where I got about nine hours of sleep. I paid for the lodging with part of the money that I carried around my waist in a money belt that my mother insisted I wear.

The next morning, I had a breakfast of fresh grapefruit, ham and eggs, hot oatmeal and coffee. Now that I was rested, well fed and clear thinking, I still had no plan. But one thing I had to do was call my mother. I had promised to call her at least once a week during our travels. Ever since my dad died, almost three years ago, Mom has been supporting us by working as the manager in a real-estate sales office. Of course, I have always loved her, but in the last three years we have become very close. I made a collect call to her office in Riverside.

After accepting the telephone charges, she greeted me, "Hello, Grant. How are you?"

"Fine, Mom. I'm calling from San Diego."

"Yes, I know. The operator told me."

"How are things at home?"

"Quite normal. Grandpa broke his thumb when he fell down while roller-skating."

"I didn't know that Grandpa roller-skated."

"He's had a very short career. It began at one o'clock Saturday and ended at one forty-five. He's talking about taking up water-skiing, as soon as his thumb heals."

"Great. Everybody should have a hobby."

Mom chuckled. We spoke about the weather and assorted inconsequential things. Then just before we said good-bye, Mom said, "Janice's mother, Mrs. Gleason, called me and asked if you had found Janice."

"Not yet."

"Mrs. Gleason also said that her sister in San Diego may be able to help. Her name is Mrs. Alan Barbor."

"I'll call her."

"Good-bye, dear. And don't forget to dress warmly and don't get a chill."

"It's eighty-five degrees here."

"That has nothing to do with it, I'm only doing my duty as a mother."

"Love you, Mom."

I looked up the telephone number of Alan Barbor and dialed it. A woman's voice answered: "Hello?"

"Is this Mrs. Barbor?"

"Yes."

"My name is Grant Decker, a friend of your niece, Janice Gleason."

"Oh. How are you?"

"I'm fine. Your sister asked me to look up Janice while I was here in San Diego."

"That's nice."

"It seems that she's worried about Janice."

"Oh, my sister is a worrywart. Everything is all right."

"You mean that you spoke to Janice?"

"No. I spoke to my son, Tommy."

"How does he know?"

"He went to look for Janice and he found her and called me."

"When was that?"

"About a month ago."

"Where is he now?"

"He's doing some religious study and charitable work."

"Where?"

"With a religious group called, I believe, 'Children of the Savior.'"

I took a moment to digest this. Things were getting complicated. Then an idea began to develop on how I might get Sally out of the Savior's compound.

"Can I come to see you, Mrs. Barbor?" I asked.

"Certainly."

She gave me directions on how to get to her home by bus. An hour later, I met Mrs. Barbor. She was a plain woman with a pleasant manner. A little bit on the heavy side. Dressed in a flower print dress.

After the usual greetings, I said, "Your sister asked me to say hello to Janice, but I haven't been able to find her. Do you think your son, Tommy, would know where she is?"

"I expect so."

"How can I meet him?"

"He's at that religious retreat that I told you about."

"Oh, yes. I'm pretty sure that's the one I visited. Do you have a picture of Tommy? So that I will know him when I meet him."

"Yes. Wait. I'll get it for you."

A few minutes later she handed me a black-and-white snapshot. Looking out of the photograph was my old bodyguard—Tobias! Except that he appeared leaner and his complexion seemed clear.

"Is this Tommy?"

She looked puzzled. "Of course. What a strange question."

"Is his middle name Tobias?"

"No."

"Does anyone call him Tobias?"

"Not that I know of. Why?"

I stood there not knowing what to say. If I told her my experience, it would probably upset her and not help solve the problem. And I wasn't too sure what, exactly, *was* the problem.

She interrupted my thoughts when she said, "When you see Tommy, tell him that we received a notice that he has to renew the registration for his car next week."

"His car?"

"Yes. He left it in our garage when he went away."

That was it! The car was the key to my getting back into the cult and rescuing Sally. And, perhaps, Janice.

"May I borrow Tommy's car for the day?"

"Of course."

Soon I was tooling along the highway in a 1980 Datsun, heading for the fun and frolic center of the Children of the Everlasting Smiles.

CHAPTER 4

It's one thing to enter the lion's den. It's quite another if the lion happens to be at home. And hungry.

I was sure that Jerry was upset when Tobias—Tommy reported my disappearance. But my second coming would gladden Jerry's heart when I revealed to him that I was returning to his fold with a five-speed Datsun as a forgiveness offering.

Tobias might not be so happy. Especially if he saw that it was his car. Since I had no solution for this dilemma, I didn't waste time worrying about it. When the time came, I'd improvise something. Or have my head broken.

In dealing with Jerry and his happy horde, it would be absolutely essential that I keep my mind clear and my thinking at least one step ahead of them. This, I felt, would be no problem, since I was convinced that they were all programmed and responded without any new or creative thoughts. Except for Jerry. He worried me. He was no programee. He was the programer. And in control.

But I had no choice. If the cards I held were lousy, they were the only cards I had.

I pulled off the main highway onto the dirt road leading to the heavenly recruiting and processing area. Rather than driving up to the front door and risk having my rescue mission come to an early and messy end when Tobias saw his car, I decided to hide it in a clump of trees a short distance down from the parking area. I parked it so that it was facing down and toward the highway. In case I had to make a hurried getaway, I didn't want to waste time demonstrating any fancy backing and turning techniques.

As I trudged up to the house, I donned my disguise: a big, vacant smile. My intention was to find Sally and to try to avoid Jerry. I remembered seeing a large tent in the rear of the house. It was almost certain that that was where the new female recruits were housed. I had to get there without being noticed or, if seen, without exciting any suspicion.

I circled around the side of the house, keeping about fifty feet between me and the house. I walked with a purposeful stride. Giving the appearance (I hoped) of being on an important mission, with no doubts about its significance or destination. I could hear singing coming from the house.

Just as I reached the rear of the house and could see the large tent, I saw a man come out of the tent and walk toward me. I didn't recognize him. I intended to ignore him and walk past. But he stopped and questioned me.

"What are you doing here?"

"Haven't you heard?"

"Heard? What?"

"I have come to bring you the news that our leader is to bring a message to us *in person,*" I enlightened him.

"Truly?"

"Do angels have wings?"

"What?"

"Never mind. The important thing is . . . are you prepared to receive him?"

"Prepared? How?"

"Are your thoughts cleansed of all things but him?"

"I . . . I don't know."

"Go then . . . immediately . . . to a quiet place . . . and meditate on his goodness."

He hesitated and looked confused.

"You hesitate, brother," I admonished him, then

continued, "I detect that doubts and evil, selfish thoughts are soiling your mind. When you doubt, you deny our leader. . . . I may have to report this."

His eyes blinked in panic.

"No, no . . . I have no doubts."

I took his hand and led him to a small clump of trees. I sat him down behind a tree and soberly advised him, "Now meditate on your soul. Do not talk to anyone. Remember, he loves you . . . and I love you."

I quickly walked away and entered the tent.

The group was singing. Led by Joshua and his hypnotizing guitar. I tried to be unobtrusive as I looked around. I recognized some of the girls who came with Sally and me on the bus. There was a scattering of young men in the group. My suspicions were that they were there to "help" the new female recruits. Then I saw Sally. Sitting cross-legged on the wooden tent floor. I cautiously worked my way toward her. Singing as I went. I sat down beside her and tapped her arm.

She turned her gaze toward me. At first, she didn't seem to recognize me. Then she smiled and said, "Hello, Grant."

"Hi, Sally."

Her eyes looked glazed. As though her mind were disconnected from her sight.

"Isn't it beautiful?" she asked.

I was surprised. But then I understood. Sally's parents were divorced when she was six years old. Her mother became a successful businesswoman. And was home very seldom. Sally was brought up by a succession of strangers. She never really felt that she had a family. She grew up bright, independent, questioning and seemingly unaffected by the lack of warmth. Now she was surrounded by all this love. It was easy to accept.

"Yes, it is beautiful, Sally," I replied.

"Abigail."

"What?"

"Abigail. That's my name now."

"Oh."

I put my arm around her and helped her to her feet, trying not to be conspicuous, and slowly walked with her to the entrance of the tent. A young fellow spotted us just as we were walking out. He hurried over. We were now outside the tent. The young man was about five feet eight and weighed about one hundred and forty pounds.

He anxiously asked Sally, "Is everything all right, sister?"

"Yes," replied Sally with that absent smile.

"Well, you shouldn't leave the sisters while we're singing," he said.

I momentarily considered flattening him with a short right to his thin jaw. But that would have stirred up a commotion that I wouldn't be able to handle. Instead I smiled an all-teeth winner and exclaimed, "Certainly, brother . . . but this is the most joyous time of our lives and we want to share it with you."

I put my arm around his shoulder and beamed at him like a father greeting a beloved son who has just returned home after a three-year absence. He tried to adjust to my enthusiasm.

"What is your name, brother?" I asked.

"Simon."

"Well, Simon, your love has saved us and I want to thank you."

I put my arms around him in a bear hug and picked him off the ground. I'm six feet one, weigh one hundred and eighty pounds, and my high-school football workouts have given me a healthy pair of arms.

"I love you, Simon," I gushed as I squeezed his chest in my arms. He tried to smile as his eyes began to bug out. "Holding you can only express part of my joy," I explained to him as I applied some more love pressure.

He couldn't talk. I put him down and showered him with my top-of-the-line smile. Then I asked, "May I hug you again, dear brother? I want your pure soul close to me."

Simon backed away. Gasping. I walked toward him.

"Don't deny me . . . now that we have found each other."

Sally was watching without any show of emotion. Simon staggered back into the tent.

I called after him, "Come back, brother, I need you."

Simon had all the needing that he could handle for the day.

There was no time to waste. By now, someone in authority or control must have been alerted to the slightly unusual occurrences taking place in happyland. I took Sally's arm and said, "Come, Sally, I—"

"Abigail."

"Of course . . . Abigail. Let's go for a walk, I want to show you something."

"Everybody is so wonderful and dedicated . . . and unselfish. I didn't know that such people existed."

"I know."

"They give their lives to serving. We are lucky they've accepted us."

I nodded in agreement as we walked around the house and headed for the car. Nobody was in sight and I began to relax.

Too soon.

"Brother Grant. I'm so happy to see you."

It was Jerry's voice.

I looked around and saw him coming toward us. Smiling. He continued, "They told me that you had returned."

I matched him smile for smile and replied, "I have . . . but it was not easy."

"What do you mean?"

"Brother Tobias left me stranded in some shopping mall. But don't be too severe with him. Part of the blame is mine. It was an unfamiliar area and I became disoriented."

"Brother Tobias was sent to another station to work and do penance for his carelessness."

"I hope he forgives me," I said contritely.

"Never mind. The important thing is that you are back."

"Yes. And I brought the car with me." I put my hand in my pocket and brought out the car keys to show him. His eyes took on a new sparkle as he extended his hand to receive the keys. I put them back in my pocket and said, "Let me show you the car."

"It is not necessary."

"But it is. . . . It is important to show you what I once prized so dearly . . . and now my greatest joy will be to give it to our leader."

Jeremiah was not easy to con. He eyed me warily. But he could find no reason not to go along with me. At least for a while. I looked around quickly. No one was in sight. This was a mistake. I later found out that Jerry doesn't move around without a bodyguard nearby. We started to walk down the path to the car.

"I was just telling Sister Abigail about the joy of giving . . . trying to persuade her to do likewise," I said.

"Oh."

"Yes. She has a savings account that is of no use to her now."

Now Jerry had something else to think about.

"She must only give of her own free will," observed Jerry smoothly.

Soon we were standing near the tree under which the gold-colored Datsun was parked. I glanced at Sally. She could not make sense out of my talk of giving a car to her new friends. She knew that I had none.

"Do not speak, sister. I realize that your emotions are confused. Soon it will all become clear."

Jerry was eyeing the car with satisfaction.

"A worthy gift," he said.

If I were alone, I could push Jerry aside, jump in the car, start it and drive off. But I had no idea what Sally's reaction would be when I tried to get her into the car. I would need more time. There was only one possibility.

We were standing at the rear of the car. Admiring it. I took the keys out of my pocket, put them in my left hand and extended them toward Jerry.

"Now I can give it to you, brother."

As he reached for them, I measured the distance between us carefully, then cocked my right fist and drove it into his jaw. With some pleasure, I'm afraid. He went down like a ripe apple falling from a tree.

A second later, I felt a tremendous blow to the top of my head. I collapsed to my knees. My God, I thought, Sally is coming to Jerry's aid and is about to crack my skull. I put my hand to my head and felt the wetness that I knew must be blood. Turning my head, I looked over my shoulder and saw a fellow standing over me, brandishing a short, heavy tree limb. Ready to hit me again. I fell to the ground and tried to roll away from the coming blow.

At that moment, Sally came up to Jerry's avenger, set herself, and then delivered a short karate chop, with the edge of her open hand, to his throat. His career as a head basher came to an abrupt end. He joined Jerry on the ground smelling the fallen pine needles. And gasping.

Something must have momentarily snapped in Sally's mind when she saw the club crack down on my head. And made her react almost instinctively.

She looked down at the groaning bodyguard and murmured, in anguish, "Oh, God, what did I do?"

I struggled to my feet. "It's all right. Don't worry, they'll be fine," I assured her.

I maneuvered her to the passenger side of the car, opened the door and helped her into the car, then slammed the door. I rushed around to the driver's side, got in and started the car.

Soon we were speeding down the highway. Not talking. My head ached from the blow and the question that filled it: When, if ever, would Abigail become Sally again?

CHAPTER 5

And there were other problems. Our backpacks, sleeping bags and changes of clothing were left at the camp of our former gracious hosts. I briefly considered telephoning Jerry to ask him if he would be a dear chap and forward our stuff to a freight depot in San Diego. But I was afraid that he might construe the punch to his jaw as something personal. Even so, forgiving is usually a big item in religious and moral philosophies. And Jerry could consider forgiving and forgetting this incident to be a test of his virtue. But the chances were that he would flunk the test.

I glanced at Sally. She was sitting quietly. Her eyes seemed to be staring and unfocused. Which, I suppose, is to be expected after four days of practically no sleep, eating junk food and being drowned in the paralyzing beat of high-volume musical noise. And being subjected to a campaign of "love bombing."

After the mass suicide at Jonestown in Guyana, I read a book on religious cults, so I had a slight understanding of what must be going on in her head. But I was far from certain. I was worried that the wrong words or actions on my part would deepen her confusion and do more harm.

"How do you feel?" I asked.

"Very upset. Why did you hit Brother Jeremiah?"

"I don't know. Something came over me."

"We must apologize to him."

"Yes."

We were quiet for a while.

39

"Where did you get this car?" she asked.

"I borrowed it from Janice Gleason's aunt. Did you talk to or see Janice?"

"No. She's at another ashram."

There was a deadness in her voice. The Sally of less than a week ago had a quick mind, a penetrating intelligence and a beautiful sense of humor.

"Where are we going?"

"I have to return the car."

"Oh. . . . When are we going back to our friends?"

I was tempted to say "when chickens talk and pigs fly." But I replied, "As soon as possible."

Soon I pulled up in front of the Barbor home and parked the car.

Sally and I were greeted cheerfully by Mrs. Barbor. I introduced Sally. "Mrs. Barbor, this is"—I hesitated—"Abigail, a friend of Janice's."

Mr. Barbor came into the room. He was a short man with wavy gray hair and alert dark eyes. He was wearing a navy blue cardigan sweater over a white shirt and a neatly pressed pair of dark trousers. After the round of introductions, he asked, "Did you see Tommy?"

"No. He went to another location," I answered.

"I'm worried about him. Those people are up to no good."

"Don't be silly, Alan. He's doing wonderful things. And not getting into trouble or using drugs like those other kids," Mrs. Barbor assured him.

Mr. Barbor didn't seem convinced. Then she turned to us and asked, "Did you have dinner yet?"

"No."

"Please stay and eat. There's plenty of food."

"Thank you. That's very kind of you."

"Oh, it's a pleasure to have young people around. Tommy was the last of the children at home. Our daughters are married."

The meal was delicious. Soup, roast chicken, fresh broccoli, a green salad and apple pie with a slice of cheese. The conversation during the dinner was about our friendship with Janice, the difference between the weather back home in Riverside and the weather in San Diego and what we expected to do with our lives after college. During the latter part of the conversation, Sally fell silent. Several times she started to say something but some inner debate seemed to make it difficult for her to express herself.

"Where are you staying?" asked Mr. Barbor.

"With the Children of the Savior. We've been with them for a while now," replied Sally.

The Barbors looked at us. Mystified.

Before things became too confusing to explain, I said, "Yes. But we're not returning immediately. There are a few things that I have to clear up."

"That's where Tommy is," exclaimed Mrs. Barbor, oblivious to any problem.

"Yes, I know," I acknowledged. And frantically tried to think of ways to change the trend of the conversation.

Mr. Barbor looked at us. Then nodded his head as if agreeing with his own unspoken thought. He looked directly at me. I was sure that he understood.

"Of course, of course . . . Bess, ask the young people if they want tea or coffee or maybe a Diet Pepsi," Mr. Barbor suggested.

After we had finished our drinks, Mr. Barbor said, "We have two empty bedrooms and we'd be happy if you two stayed here with us tonight."

I looked at Sally. She seemed indifferent. I accepted his kind offer.

"Thank you. That would be perfect," I said.

Until bedtime, Mr. Barbor and I kept the conversation away from the Children of the Savior.

Sally slept for about ten hours. The next morning she was more alert and more like herself. But if I was hoping for everything to be as it was before our experience, I was disappointed. After a healthy breakfast, Sally turned to me and said, "Grant, I know

41

that you are delaying going back to the Children. I'm not sure of the reason, but it must be that there are doubts in your mind. But I'm going back and I'd like you to come with me."

I felt sick. I was losing Sally. And worse than that, I was convinced that Sally was losing herself. But as she spoke, an idea was taking shape in my mind that might have a chance of getting her to see things more objectively. Or, at least, how they appeared to me.

"You're right, Sally . . . er, Abigail."

"It doesn't matter. You can call me Sally, if you want to."

"I do have doubts."

"But why? The Children want to work together to do good things. The world that we grew up in is selfish, self-centered and destructive. With no real meaning. . . . Oh, I know that there are a lot of good people . . . but they are not *doing* anything. This is our chance to set an example."

The strange thing was that she made more than a little sense.

"Please give me a few days and help me clear up my doubts," I said.

"All right. I'm sure that I can convince you," said Sally.

She sounded like an evangelist about to make her first convert.

I knew that simply to argue with Sally would not convince her. There was no way that you could attack their ideals. After all, what was bad about loving your fellow man? And devoting yourself to helping him?

It would be easier to denounce motherhood.

The only way to convince Sally that she was looking at a carefully prepared illusion designed to appeal to her ideals would be to show her what they actually *did*. Rather than what they said.

The Barbors were extemely generous. They said

that we could use Tommy's car to run errands or do some sight-seeing. But for the first phase, the car would not be necessary. I found out that there was a local library about three miles from the Barbor home.

Sally has a beautiful body, which she keeps exquisitely tuned with athletics. She earned a brown belt in karate, and was the star and played singles on the high-school tennis team. I enjoyed football, tennis and, occasionally, mixing it up in the boxing ring.

"Sally, I'd like to do some jogging to help clear my head. Will you come with me?" I asked.

"That's a good idea," she replied.

"We can head for the library. There's some stuff that I want to look up."

CHAPTER 6

I'm not sure why it is so, but I find that strenuous exercise has a way of reducing my worries and freeing my mind to grapple more effectively with a problem.

As we were jogging to the library at a fairly fast pace, I felt less tense and more certain that I could persuade Sally that she was being mentally manipulated.

Of course, the other side of that coin was that Sally was perhaps becoming more convinced that she had been shown the light and could convince *me* of its truth.

But, no matter what the outcome, I knew that I could never leave Sally. If she went back to the Children, I would go with her.

"Why do you want to go to the library?" asked Sally.

"Well, if we're going to live and work with the Children, I'd like to know more about them."

"But they told us everything."

"Maybe."

Sally was silent for a minute. Then she said, "It is important to have faith."

I detected some uneasiness in her voice and decided to press her a little.

"But faith should have some basis. It can't be sustained on hot air."

She didn't answer.

I continued, "I'm sure that you're not afraid of examining this thing closely. There's an old saying:

44

'The truth doesn't fear the critical eye of the skeptic.' "

That "old saying" was composed two seconds before. In my head. But it sounded like something that Socrates might have laid on one of his pupils.

We were soon at the library. It was a large one and appeared to be well stocked. After consulting the catalog, I gathered seven books on cults, thought reform, mind control and brainwashing.

We sat down at a study table in a corner of the library and started to read. I soon found myself roaming through a strange world. The world of the cults. Because of the mass suicides in Guyana and the subsequent newspaper coverage, I was dimly aware of their existence. But I had no idea of their variety and extent.

All of the cults have a living leader who has absolute authority over its members. The cults promise to save the world but do almost nothing to benefit the communities from which they extract their income. The evidence indicates that there are more than 1700 cults in the U.S. with a total membership of more than one million.

The recruits in these groups are not off-the-wall misfits but sons and daughters of the sturdy middle class, usually with some college experience. They are filled with ideals and are looking for answers to the complex problems of growing up in a confused and confusing world. The cults offer a seemingly safe, protected life, where like-minded young people are working together for a common and worthy goal.

The only trouble is that the leaders of most of the cults use the organizations for personal power trips. And some of them live in lavish styles, supported by the earnings of their unpaid members living in poverty and acting as psychological slaves.

Many of the cults use deceptive recruiting techniques and keep the recruits enthralled with emotional and physical pressures that are loosely termed "brainwashing." The more accepted description of their method is "coercive persuasion."

As I read and began to understand the agony and confusion that Sally was undergoing, I clung to one ray of hope. It was that Sally had been subjected to their persuasive influence for only a short length of time.

Sally started to read the books casually and almost with indifference. She just turned the pages and glanced at an occasional paragraph. But it wasn't long before something caught her eye and she began to read carefully and with close attention.

Soon I heard her mutter something to herself. "Oh, Wow!"

I looked up and asked, "Did you say something?"

"Yes. Here's a description of exactly what they did to me."

"Oh . . . what was that?"

" 'Sleep deprivation . . . constant surveillance . . . sustained sensory input with endless music, speeches, exhortations, criticism and promises . . . 'love bombing' . . . no time or energy left to think or be critical.' " She exploded. "They sure did a number on me."

"Yeah . . . but they promised some good stuff," I reminded her.

Sally looked at me.

"They're good kids and I like them. Maybe even love them. All they want to do is to help others and to live a meaningful life."

"Doesn't sound bad."

"Of course not. The ends are beautiful."

"So?"

"The means stink . . . now keep quiet and let me read."

The physical rest and mental stimulation of the books had released the critical capacities of Sally's mind. We read for about two hours. It was one helluva revelation. Toward the end, Sally was shaking her head in disbelief and building up a store of anger.

"Do you know what?" she asked.

"What?"

"The Moonies are estimated to be worth hundreds of millions of dollars, with an annual American income of sixty million dollars."

"Wow!"

"And a Moonie organization is an important defense contractor in South Korea. It manufactures air rifles and parts for the M-79 grenade launcher and vulcan gun."

"Just your basic religious goods."

"Not funny."

I kept quiet. Finally Sally closed the books and stared ahead. Lost in thought.

"Those pyramids were great pieces of work," she said.

"What?"

"The Egyptian pyramids . . . they were built to please the gods and to enable the pharaohs to sail into heaven, smiling and chanting all the way."

"Oh."

"I would hate to have been one of the slaves who built the pyramids," she said.

"How about being one of the servants who were buried alive with the heaven-going pharaoh?"

"If it weren't for the honor of the thing, I would have preferred going out for a pizza and a Seven-Up," replied Sally.

In one of the books, I came across a quote that summed up the philosophy of a self-appointed moral leader. He was advising another aspiring Pied Piper. He said, "Do you know when God's saying to move on to the next town? When you can turn people on their head and shake them and no money falls out, then you know God's saying, 'Move on, Son.'"

We left the library and jogged back to the Barbor house.

CHAPTER 7

Sally quickly regained her independent spirit and her healthy skepticism. Some anger remained. She resented the dishonesty and the manipulative techniques used to exploit her idealism. But more than that she was disturbed by the condition of the kids caught in that mind-numbing organization. Most of them were gentle, caring souls who were seeking to love and be loved.

Our friend Janice was that type. She was plain-looking but had a sweetness that came through to anybody who knew her. She was intelligent and her greatest pleasure seemed to be in helping others.

It's strange how I keep using the past tense whenever I think of her. As if she no longer existed. She was supposed to graduate from high school at the same time as Sally and I.

Janice's telephone call to Sally announcing her impending marriage to a phantom and her rejection of her parents seemed unnatural and disturbing at the time. In the light of our short experience with the cult, it now appeared ominous and almost criminal.

There was no way that we could walk away and leave Janice under the control of those sanctimonious hypocrites.

But what could we do? Her aunt, Mrs. Barbor, didn't think there was any real problem. She kept telling her sister that "it's nice that Janice is involved in spiritual work." Her uncle was becoming increasingly worried, however. Especially now that his son, Tommy, had become involved.

"Did you find out anything about Janice?" I asked Sally the day after our trip to the library.

"Not much. Her name is now Grace and she was sent to work at another temple or camp about three hours away from here."

"Do you know the name of the place?"

"They kept referring to it as 'Bethel' . . . I think that it's an estate near the town of Dundeen."

We were both silent for a minute, then Sally said, "If we don't do something she's lost."

I nodded in agreement. "We'll have to call her parents and tell them what we *know* . . . but I don't think it's a good idea to scare them with our guess about the future."

Sally agreed.

Before calling Janice's parents, we told the Barbors about our experiences at the Children of the Savior enclave. I told them that I had seen Tommy, now called Tobias, but could not tell them where he was now staying. Mrs. Barbor still did not take her son's situation seriously but Mr. Barbor vowed to take a trip to the camp and demand some answers.

I had the feeling that he would get a lot of answers but none of them straight.

The next day there was a new development: the Gleasons called and said that Janice's brother, Harold, was on his way to California.

We picked him up at the airport that evening. He was very agitated. He was more than agitated. He was angry and determined to rescue his sister. Harold is twenty—two years older than Janice—about five feet eight, slightly built and studying accounting at college. Unlike a lot of brothers and sisters, Janice and he were very close all through their childhood.

He showed us a letter that he had received. A few sentences were so unusual and outrageous that they stuck in my mind: "I fled before Satan could confuse me and force me to live with the comforts of the flesh. . . . This flesh will pass away but the soul will survive with my true parents. . . . They are not my true parents . . . only those of this flesh . . . we live by faith and give no thought to what we eat, drink or wear. . . . There is a great deal of persecution to endure.''

The letter was signed "Grace."

Harold was convinced that because they had been so close, he could bring Janice back to her senses.

Sally and I had doubts on two counts. First, we felt that he would not be allowed to talk to her alone. This was one of the cult's techniques. A member is never allowed to meet or talk to outsiders without having at least one other cult member present. Second, Harold was not emotionally or intellectually equipped to deal with Janice's psychological state. This would require a professional working in a favorable environment over a period of time. None of these conditions would exist on the cult's home grounds. They owned the territory and made the rules.

We explained this to Harold. He seemed to understand but would not change his mind. He was determined to go in and try. The final unpleasant possibility was that he would go in and not come out. He pooh-poohed this idea as being ridiculous. Sally and I gave up trying to talk him out of his plan.

Instead we decided to join him—after taking certain precautions and safeguards.

The idea was somewhat scary and, from what we already knew, more than a little dangerous. But Harold's determination and Janice's strange letter were drawing us into the project.

Our best weapon and strongest defense in resisting surrender to the cult was our knowledge of their methods and purpose. In addition, we planned a method of monitoring each other and an escape route, if needed.

The more we talked about it, the clearer it became.

Our basic mission would be to gather as much inside information as possible about the operation of the cult.

Equally important, we would try to persuade Janice to leave. If we didn't succeed within a week, we would get out.

By now, even Mrs. Barbor was worried. She had seen the letter from Janice and had not been able to contact her son, Tommy. Mr. Barbor was so aggravated that he wanted to come with us. We talked him out of that idea.

Our next move was to buy cheap backpacks for each of us and to put in some extra socks and underwear as well as a large supply of vitamin pills and protein diet supplements. The Barbors and Harold thought that the vitamins were silly and tried to talk us out of them. I was insistent and quoted my grandmother's favorite expression, "it can't hurt," as my authority.

I went to the library and checked back issues of the regional newspapers and gathered what information was available on Bethel, the place where we expected to find Janice.

The three of us loaded into a car that Harold rented, and began our rescue mission.

CHAPTER 8

On the drive to Bethel we reviewed the information that we had gathered about our destination and its people. Bethel was the shining light in the "Savior of the Children" organization. It produced more money than any of the other branches and was run by a dynamic former encyclopedia salesman who called himself "Prophet Anselm." Using Bethel as a home base, teams of members would go out in vans on selling pilgrimages to raise money. They sold flowers, peanuts and candy. Bethel itself was a millionaire's estate that was bought by the group three years ago.

About five miles from Bethel was the small town of Dundeen. We reached there about noon and parked the car in a garage. The rest of the journey would be on foot. Each of us hid one hundred dollars in our socks. A fifty-dollar bill in each sock.

While walking, Sally and I reviewed the indoctrination methods used by the group. These included sleep deprivation, constant assault on the senses, no privacy, endless proclamations of love, a diet high in starch and sugar, and appeals to faith and goodness. Harold listened but seemed to think that he was immune.

We then decided on a method that would check whether or not the pressure of the group and its techniques were beginning to have an effect on one of us, consciously or unconsciously. Because, whether Harold believed it or not, there were cases of people who, while investigating a cult and thinking that they would not be affected by the psychological forces surrounding them, wound up becoming members.

We planned on using two defense measures. First, we would try to stay together as much as possible. Second, and more important, at least twice each day we would pass each other a magic phrase and a response. A phrase that no true believer could utter.

The phrase was "The Prophet stinks." The response was "Yea, verily, the Prophet stinks."

It was inconceivable to us that anybody could be a believer and deliver the phrase with any conviction. If there was any hesitation by one of us in giving the golden phrase or response, it would be time to break out of the funny farm.

After an hour of walking along a secondary road out of Dundeen, we came to some high steel fencing set back fifty feet from the road on the right side. Then we saw a tall gate made of ornamental iron supported by stone columns on either side. A small plaque on one of the columns announced:

S.O.C.

Private Property

KEEP OUT

The gate was open and no guards seemed near.

"S.O.C. must stand for 'Savior of the Children,'" said Sally.

"This is the place," I agreed.

"Let us give praise and enter."

We all shook hands and each gave our solemn oath.

"The Prophet stinks."

"Yea, verily, the Prophet stinks."

Harold sounded a little sheepish and looked around as if afraid that somebody would hear us.

After passing through the gate, we walked along a tree-lined road that was paved with bluestone chips. A quarter of a mile into the estate the road forked into two paths. The right fork led to a locked gate. Beyond the gate, up a short hill, we could see a large Tudor-style mansion. As we were looking at the elegant building, two large Dobermans came racing down the hill. Barking as they came. When they reached the gate, they stopped barking and bared their teeth and snarled.

"Did you bring any raw meat with you?" asked Sally.

"No."

"Then I suggest that we take the other road."

"Good thinking."

We trudged up the road on the left. The dogs must have alerted the people ahead of us because within a minute we saw two people approaching us. A clean-shaven young man with a short haircut and a young woman with long blond hair, wearing a simple white cotton dress.

The fellow asked, "Can I help you?"

"Yes," I replied. "I'm Grant, this is Sally and this is Harold . . . and you are . . . ?"

"Zelig."

"Mighty glad to meet you, Zelig. We've been on the road a long time . . . and we're very tired but happy to be here."

"Where do you think you are?" asked Zelig.

"This is Bethel, isn't it? Where the Children of the Savior live?"

"Yes."

"Well, we've come to offer our services in whatever way we can."

"How do you know about Bethel?"

"Oh, how stupid of me. I'm so tired that I'm not thinking straight . . . I should have told you right away. Harold's sister, Grace, lives here and she's written him about the glorious work that you are doing."

"Oh."

"And if it's true, it's the kind of thing that Sally and I have been looking for since we left home."

"Left home?"

"We're not proud of it . . . but it was what we had to do. I don't know if you can understand, but we think there's more to life than becoming cogs in a mindless machine and having no real meaning. I'm embarrassed to say it, but I mean without any . . . er . . . spiritual meaning."

"Don't be embarrassed."

Zelig's defenses seemed to lower. He turned to the girl standing next to him and said, "Tabitha, let's take these good people to see Anselm."

As we started up the road, Sally engaged Zelig in conversation. "It's so peaceful here, except for those frightening dogs. Whose lovely house is that on the hill?" She indicated the mansion guarded by the dogs.

"The Savior stays there when he comes to bless us with his presence."

"How nice."

Soon we came to a clearing and a complex of buildings. There was a small residence that I took to be the home of the former caretaker of the estate. Then there was a one-story building about two hundred feet long that had probably once been horse stables. Lastly there was a large barnlike structure that I later found out had been an indoor riding rink. When it was raining or too cold for the millionaire and his friends to go horseback riding outdoors, they pounded the saddles with their rumps by riding indoors.

Parked in the center of the complex were ten to twelve beat-up vans, Fords, Chevys, Dodges, etc., with no identifying marks on them.

Zelig led us to the caretaker's house. This was evidently where Prophet Anselm hung out. He opened the front door and motioned us in. Tabitha had disappeared. We went in and waited for Zelig to come in and close the door. After he entered, he walked over to a door just to the right of the entrance hall. He knocked and a voice called out.

"Come in."

He opened the door, stood in the doorway and said, "I have three wanderers from the outside. May I bring them in to meet you?"

"Certainly, Brother Zelig."

We all entered. Anselm was sitting in a leather swivel chair behind a large desk. He was a dapper man with wavy gray hair, wearing a three-piece, banker-gray business suit.

"Welcome," he said as he stood up and shook our hands.

Zelig introduced us.

"What is your desire?" asked Anselm.

I ran the rap about the letter from Grace and leaving home and wandering around looking for spiritual meaning and hoping to find really useful work. He seemed to think that this was perfectly normal. It was even starting to make sense to me.

When I had finished, Anselm said, "The Savior can always use willing hands." Then he turned to Zelig and asked, "Is Sister Grace here today?"

"Yes."

"Please fetch her."

A few minutes later Janice was ushered in. She was much heavier than when I had last seen her and her complexion was covered with tiny pimples. She was wearing a smile that didn't involve her eyes. She looked at Harold for a moment, didn't seem to recognize him, then burst out, "Harold."

But didn't move.

Harold went to her and hugged her. I watched him nervously, afraid that he would blow the whole deal by saying how worried their parents were and to come home. To prevent that I spoke up.

"Grace, you look so happy."

She looked at me, then at Sally, and recognized us.

"Grant . . . Sally."

"We heard about the great things you are doing and hope to join you."

Anselm beamed and said, "Sister Grace is one of our best workers and brings much joy to the Savior and me."

Janice-Grace bowed her head in humbleness.

Anselm continued, "And now, miracle of miracles, the Savior has sent us three souls to replace the two who were weakened by Satan."

Grace nodded. I couldn't figure out what Anselm was talking about but it soon became clear.

Anselm asked, "Tell me, Sister Grace, how do we know when Satan is in our souls?"

"When we come home before we have earned our quota of heavenly gifts."

"Yes . . . and for three days now, two of the sisters in your fund-raising team have returned with almost half of their heavenly merchandise unsold. There is no surer sign than this of the workings of Satan."

Holy Guru! This was a dynamite concept in sales management. If the salesman doesn't make his quota it's because he's messing around with the devil. Wait till General Motors hears about this.

"As you know, Sister Grace, I'm sending the two sisters to Elysium to receive help in fighting Satan and to strengthen their faith."

Elysium was the location where Sally and I had our experience with Jerry and his troops.

"Sally and Grant will be their replacements," continued Anselm. "Take them under your capable wings and teach them how to earn heavenly donations."

Grace lowered her head in acknowledgment.

Turning to Zelig, Anselm said, "Harold will be in

your care." He smiled and dismissed us with, "That will be all."

As we were leaving, a final thought occurred to him. "I will give you your true names tomorrow. Meantime, you may use the ones you came with."

Thanks, Pops.

CHAPTER 9

Grace and Zelig led us across the parking area to the stables. The very long, one-story building had been converted to living quarters for the sisters and brothers, the workers in this beehive of heavenly commerce. The women occupied one end of the building and the men the other end.

Harold and I went with Zelig, while Sally was led away by Grace. Seeing his sister had made Harold tense. He had difficulty restraining himself from talking to her. I was sure her changed appearance worried him. I tried to reassure him.

"Patience, brother," I cautioned as I put a calming hand on his shoulder.

As we entered the building, I heard music coming from a public address system, flooding the interior. In the center of the building, on the concrete floor, were seated about thirty young men. They were in the lotus position and had their eyes closed.

Along each side of the building the original partitions that formed the stalls for the horses still stood. The stalls were now sleeping areas for the occupants. There were rolled-up sleeping bags in some places. Others had blankets spread over heaps of straw. Most of the sections had wooden produce crates, standing on their ends, serving as shelves to hold the few personal belongings of the residents—toothbrushes in glasses, shaving equipment, soap, folded towels, etc. It appeared that each stall housed two or three people.

Harold and I were not put in the same pen. I knew

from my reading that separating us was part of the technique in maintaining control of new recruits. After we deposited our backpacks in our respective areas, Zelig told us to join the silent group that was meditating, or something, in the center of the building.

We sat cross-legged on the cool floor as loud, organlike music filled the building. Soon the insistent sound had its effect. I felt isolated and surrounded by the imprisoning vibrations.

I didn't close my eyes and when I looked around, I saw several of the brothers with their heads slumped forward. No longer meditating but dozing. One or two were snoring and drooling. Two monitors were walking around watching for unauthorized sleepers. Whenever they saw one they would go to him, poke him and say, "Satan is casting a spell. Drive him out!"

The head of the pokee would jerk up and he would assume an erect posture.

About five minutes after I sat down, the music stopped and a voice came over the loud speaker: "This is the Prophet Anselm blessing you and asking you to give thanks to the Savior for the joys he brings us."

I had a mental image of Anselm dressed in his banker's three-piece suit, sitting in his leather swivel chair, holding a hand microphone as he broadcast his holy sales pitch from his comfortable office.

Then the atmosphere changed to that of a tent revival meeting as Anselm's voice raised in exhortation.

"Repeat after me . . . I will never leave you."

"I will never leave you!" shouted the group in unison.

"For I have found in your bright eye . . ."

"For I have found in your bright eye . . ." they repeated.

"A river of love . . ."

"A river of love . . ."
"A heart of gold . . ."
"A heart of gold . . ."
"A peaceful mind . . ."
"A peaceful mind . . ."
"A hand to hold . . ."
"A hand to hold . . ."
"Amen."
"Amen."

Nutty as it sounds, I began to repeat the words.

Then Anselm went into high gear. By alternately raising his voice and then dropping it to a whisper, he played tunes on the emotions of his listeners. Soon all of them were glassy-eyed and shouting "Amen," "Praise be" and cries whose meanings I could not make out.

"We're building a kingdom of love."

"Praise be."

"Just my Savior and me."

"Amen."

"We're flying together as one family."

By now they really were flying. But Anselm wasn't through. He went into overdrive and laid on the serious stuff.

"We're going to have a victory for you today, Savior."

"Today . . . today."

"We're going to raise money for our Savior."

"Yes . . . yes."

"We're going to take money away from Satan."

Everybody raised their fists over their head, shook them and screamed, "Victory over Satan."

This was followed by a blast of organ music. Then Anselm commanded, "Go, my children . . . you may play a game of 'Savior Tag' to prepare your body and spirits for the struggle. Go."

Everybody stood up and trooped toward the exit. Once outside they stood around in an open area waiting for the signal to start the game. It may not replace "Ring-A-Leevio" but it was one wild scene.

One of Anselm's lieutenants started the game.

"I'm the Savior!" he shouted, then ran after one of the fellows and tagged him. Everybody else scattered. The fellow who was tagged yelled, "I'm your disciple." Whereupon he joined hands with the "Savior" and the two of them chased after somebody else. When the third person was tagged, he too became a disciple, joining hands with the other two and chasing another lost soul.

The rest of them ran around the courtyard like crazed chickens, yelling, "False Prophet." "Heresy." "Heathen." "Communist." Until they were tagged.

The last person out was Satan.

I wound up being Satan. Fortunately, I was rescued from spending an eternity in Hell by allowing myself to be tagged. And saved.

Hallelujah.

Then they played another maniacal game called "Spirit World Dodge Ball."

After that it was time for the evening meal that preceded loading into the vans for a sales pilgrimage.

The fascinating thing about the meal was that it was served by the sisters. In the world of the Savior, women are subservient to men.

This was sure to make a big hit with Sally.

The women brought buckets of macaroni and cheese, loaves of white bread, bowls of lettuce with a strange dressing and big bottles of carbonated, sweet soda.

The men lined up with paper plates and plastic forks, while the women dished out the food. They ate after the men. I saw Sally handing out the bread.

I approached her. She smiled, bowed her head and said, "Let us give thanks for the Savior's bread, brother."

It was magic-word time. Quietly I said, "The Prophet stinks."

Sally smiled sweetly and answered quietly, "Yea, verily, the Prophet will be dipped and flipped in rancid oil."

Thank heavens, her mind was still clear as a bell.

CHAPTER 10

When we had finished eating and the women had cleaned the serving bowls and utensils and disposed of the paper plates and the plastic forks, everybody assembled in teams of five or six in the central area near the vans. Each team was composed of both men and women.

Harold and I stood around not knowing what to do. Then we saw Grace, Sally and a young man approaching us. When they reached us, the young man asked, "Brother Harold?"

"Yes," replied Harold.

"Please come with me. I'll introduce you to your pilgrimage leader."

Harold and his guide walked off.

Grace was smiling.

"That's Brother Caleb. He's our leader . . . and a wonderful inspiration and teacher."

"I'm sure he is . . . and you must have learned a lot," remarked Sally.

"Oh, yes."

"Your parents will be glad to hear that."

Grace's face went blank. Then she quietly answered, "We don't talk about our physical parents."

We were on dangerous ground and Caleb was returning. Sally saw the problem and scurried to safe ground. She smiled and said, "Now you can teach us."

Caleb rejoined us and introduced himself. Then he said, "Tonight we are going to make a bar run."

"Bar run?" I asked.

"Yes . . . we are going to raise heavenly donations in bars, night spots and roadhouses."

"Sounds exciting."

"Sister Grace and I will show you what to do . . . meantime, here is the other member of our team."

Caleb turned to a small, thin, young woman with large dark eyes who had just joined us and was standing quietly just behind and to the side of Caleb. "This is Sister Prudence."

Just then, Anselm's voice boomed out of a loud speaker: "Brothers and sisters . . . it is time to mount up and charge into Satan's lair . . . and relieve him of his power . . . his money . . . so that the Savior can put it to blessed use."

He sounded like John Wayne ordering the cavalry to get humping and bring back fresh Indian scalps.

One thing surprised me and that was that Anselm was sending out new, untried, untrained recruits on a selling mission. Namely, Sally, Harold and me. I wondered about it and sought to get an answer from Caleb.

"Brother Caleb."

"Yes?"

"I think you should know that neither Sister Sally nor I have any experience in this type of mission."

"Yes, I know. The Prophet has told me . . . and he has expressed his faith in your ability to follow my lead in our struggle against Satan. To put it in worldly terms, Anselm feels that salesmanship is an innate talent."

"Oh."

"And he is putting you to the test."

"What if we fail?"

Caleb smiled and answered.

"We do not think about failure."

I subsequently found out that Anselm's consuming drive was to produce money for the cause. He didn't care diddly squat about how it was done as long as it was done. In a relatively short time, he had

66

become the fastest rising star in the organization and was very close to the Savior. Who had an enormous appreciation for large lumps of money.

If you didn't make your quota, Anselm assigned you to shoveling horse manure or he sent you to another ashram, or whatever they call the sect's branch locations.

"Let's go," ordered Caleb as he headed for an old Ford van. The van had only two seats, one for the driver and one next to the driver.

"You sit there," Caleb said to me, pointing to the seat on the passenger side.

"No, no . . . let one of the girls sit there," I protested.

"Do as I say," ordered Caleb.

Then I realized that this was part of women's secondary position. They had to ride in the back of the bus. On uncomfortable cushions, surrounded by the flowers that were to be sold.

After Caleb started the van and headed it down the road, he reached over to the dashboard and flipped a switch on a cassette player. Anselm's voice began to bounce around inside the van.

That dude never gives up.

"My thoughts are with you, brothers and sisters, as you go into battle . . ."

Then he went into a ten-minute pep talk about selling and bringing joy to the Savior. The talk was followed by some inspirational music and then a sermon on how the Savior cleansed the dirty money that we snatched from Satan.

There was no napping in the van.

About forty-five minutes down the road, we came to a truck stop. One part of it was a restaurant, and connected to the restaurant was a bar. Caleb pulled the van into a parking space. He walked to the back of the van and opened the rear doors. The three women jumped out. Caleb reached into the van and took out bunches of long-stemmed carnations. He handed one bunch to Grace and one to Prudence. He told Sally to go with the two girls and watch and listen carefully as they "blitzed" the restaurant. Then he took a bunch of flowers for himself and told me to come with him into the bar.

There were about eight men and three women sitting on stools along the bar. Another ten people were sitting at small tables around the room. Caleb took one of the flowers out of the bunch and extended it to a woman sitting near the end of the bar.

"We're soliciting donations for our work with delinquent children," he said.

The woman looked at him, not knowing how to react. The man sitting next to her asked, "How much is the flower?"

"Nothing, sir. We just hope for your donation for our charitable work."

The man reached into his pocket and said, "Give the flower to the lady." Then he gave Caleb two dollars.

"Bless you, sir."

Caleb moved rapidly down the line. About half of the people gave him money. Others looked away, somewhat embarrassed.

At one of the tables an elderly couple was seated. The man was more inquisitive than the others and asked, "What kind of work do you do?"

Without hesitation, Caleb responded, "We fight youthful drug addiction."

"Drugs are bad . . . very bad," said the man as he shook his head. He laid out five dollars for a pair of flowers. We were out of the bar in ten minutes with twenty-five dollars in Caleb's pocket. We went back to the bus and waited for the women.

Five minutes later the door to the restaurant opened and the two flower salesladies and Sally came out followed by a man in a white apron.

". . . stay out. Stop bothering my customers," he was saying.

"Bless you . . . bless you," responded Grace and Prudence.

The girls walked to the van and loaded through the rear door.

After we pulled away and were riding along the highway, Caleb reached his right hand back and the two fund-raisers put money in his open hand. They had done better than Caleb. They had gotten twenty-eight dollars.

"The Savior loves you," announced Caleb.

At the next stop Sally and I were given flowers to sell.

My sales effort got us thrown out. When a man asked me what the donation was for, I replied, "Religious work."

"What religion?"

"Children of the Savior."

"Isn't that that cult?"

"Well . . ." I didn't know what to say.

"I heard about you and I ain't giving you a cent."

The rest of the bar patrons heard this and turned to look at Caleb and me. The bartender pointed toward the door and we walked out with as much dignity as we could muster.

When we were seated in the van, Caleb told me that I must talk about "helping drug addicts," "feeding starving children," "caring for the homeless" and similar good stuff. When I looked skeptical, he said that using "heavenly deception" was necessary in fighting Satan and serving the Savior.

Also the celestial lies sold a lot more merchandise.

We continued the selling expedition until we were sold out. Which was about midnight.

By then Caleb had about eight hundred dollars stashed away. I did some quick mental calculations and figured that if the van made six runs a week, it would bring in almost five thousand dollars. And if Anselm sent out ten vans, the weekly gross would be fifty thousand dollars. Or, an annual take of two and a half million.

With a labor payroll of zip, zilch and zero.

Just feed the workers Kool-Aid, pep talks and prayers.

This was no penny-ante operation. I wondered if they taught this at Harvard Business School?

It was after one o'clock in the morning when we returned to the home stalls.

CHAPTER 11

At five-thirty the next morning, a bugle sounded over the public address system in the stable. It shocked me out of a deep sleep and scared the living daylights out of me. When I realized where I was and what was happening, I covered my ears with my arms and tried to get more sleep. Somebody began to shake me. There was no way that I could ignore the creep so I got up with a groan.

There were two bathrooms for about thirty men. A lot of the guys lined up to use them. Some fellows had gotten buckets of cold water and were splashing their faces and upper bodies. I got to use one of the bathrooms.

After our morning ablutions, we cleaned and straightened the stalls. During all of this, the loud speaker never let up pounding out inspirational noise. It was as if you were shrunk to the size of a pencil eraser and trapped inside a cassette player with no *off* switch.

Breakfast was cold, sweet cereal, bananas and milk. I managed to down some vitamin tablets.

Then came prayers and group chanting. My mind excused itself and took a walk.

At eight o'clock we loaded into the vans to start a long day of selling in offices and stores in towns whose names made no impression on me. This time we offered bags of candy and peanuts for "donations."

Several times during the day, Sally and I talked to Grace. If we spoke about the work we were doing, she responded with a practiced enthusiasm. From what she told us, I began to appreciate Anselm's creative, effective and tricky methods of shaking money out of an unsuspecting population.

She told us with pride that during the Christmas holiday, some members of the group dressed up as Santa Clauses. During Easter, they donned Easter Bunny costumes. If there was a rodeo, some of the fund-raisers put on Stetson hats and cowboy boots and gave cowboy yells to encourage donations.

However, if we attempted to talk about her previous life, Grace-Janice froze and refused to talk.

For the next few days, our fund-raising group canvassed private homes and shopping centers.

Sally, Harold and I were issued our reborn names . . . Leila, Jedediah and Lemuel.

Several times during that period, Harold tried to talk to his sister and she became very agitated. After that, members of Harold's team watched him carefully and gave him no free time to think or act by himself. Harold was beginning to acquire a dazed look.

The group worked six days a week, some days for eighteen hours, and were allowed about four hours of sleep.

Sunday was billed as a day of rest. Which meant that the fund-raising teams stayed home. The only thing the slaves *didn't* do was rest. Anselm had announced that the Savior and Mrs. Savior were coming to visit their mansion to parcel out blessings and supernal gems of inspiration.

The beehive went ape. The worker bees were hustled over to the royal hive, the mansion, and put to work cleaning, polishing, deodorizing and sanitizing the premises. Those that were not down on their knees scrubbing floors were sent to the kitchen to prepare the divine repast. But only after the pots, pans, dishes and silverware were scoured and polished free of earthly contamination.

Two other fellows and I were sent down to the food-storage area in the basement to bring up bags of potatoes, onions and fresh vegetables as well as a side of beef from which a prime steak could be cut.

It was bizarre. When I brought up the sack of onions, one of the women opened it and examined every onion in it before picking out five of them. I was fascinated.

"Why are you going through the whole bag to get five onions?" I asked.

"The Savior will only eat that which is perfect."

"Oh . . . in that case, I might as well bring up the other two sacks that are still in the basement . . . a more perfect onion may be hidden in one of them."

A look of panic came into the poor girl's eyes. I had presented her with a problem that she was not equipped to handle. She looked around for guidance but found none.

I felt sorry for her and told her, "On second thought, I'm sure that you've already picked out the five most perfect."

She looked at me in gratitude as she turned and reverently carried the onions to one of the assistant chefs.

It was the same for the rest of the food. A whole crate of oranges was inspected before a few oranges were chosen to lie in a bowl in the presence of Numero Uno and Mrs. Uno. The wildest piece of business I saw was a woman wearing white, cotton gloves cleaning a banana. With a Q-tip!

"Why are you using a Q-tip, sister?" I asked.

She looked at me with a serene smile. "Because the food must not only be physically clean but must be spiritually immaculate."

"Oh, I see . . . the old 'spirit in the Q-tip' ceremony. I should have known, sister," I said contritely.

I was given a pair of new, white, cotton gloves and told to help set the table in the dining room.

On the way to the dining room, I ran into Sally.

She was carrying some white, silk shirts over one arm. In her other hand she was clutching a quart bottle of liquid.

"Greetings, Sister Leila, to where art thou hustling thy heavenly bod?"

"Don't bug me, Brother Whatever, I've been ordered to hand-wash the head honcho's silk shirts . . . with this sanctified detergent." She waved the bottle of liquid at me.

"I've gotten fluffier laundry using New, All-Temperature, Bold-Dash," I said, trying to be helpful.

"How would you like some sanctified suds up your nose?" asked Sally.

"Bless you, sister, but I'm not yet worthy of such an honor," I replied as I hurried off to the dining room.

Four women, all wearing white gloves, were bustling around setting up the dining table. One of them was Grace. She saw me and exclaimed, "The honor of being chosen to serve is only given to a few."

The quality of the serving platters, the silver and gold flatware and the ornate hollowware was worthy of Louis XIV. That is, if old Louis could tax the peasants enough to buy the stuff.

At about six o'clock, an excited murmur ran through the house.

"He's coming up the road. He's coming up the road."

We were all assembled in the large entrance hall. Two lines were formed, one of men and one of women, to make a loving gauntlet through which the Savior would walk as he strode into the mansion.

The two front doors swung open and two women dressed in white backed into the entrance. Bowing as they came. They were followed by the Savior himself. He was of medium height and dressed in a white double-breasted suit, white shoes, white shirt and a white tie. The white of his wavy hair matched the rest of his ensemble. The effect was dramatic. The only jarring note was the potbelly that was attempting to hide under his jacket. His face had the serene smile of the very smug or very rich.

Walking behind him came a short, dark-haired woman with intense dark eyes. She was wearing a white, satin sari. I assumed that she was the Savior's lesser half.

At her side was Anselm, dressed in a pale yellow summer suit. He was grinning like an instant winner in a state lottery. They were followed by three well-dressed men in business suits. Probably the leader's lawyer and a brace of accountants.

When I looked at the faces of the Savior's followers who were lined up to greet him, I saw something strange. Many of the women and some of the men had tears running down their cheeks.

All of the disciples were bowing like extras in a low-budget Japanese movie.

The entourage stopped. Anselm looked back through the open front doors and made a beckoning motion for somebody to come in. Two male disciples entered with their arms extended in front of them, carrying something wrapped in clear plastic. I looked closely. It was a large fish. Probably tuna.

Anselm looked around proudly. "Brothers and sisters, the Savior has brought us a gift . . . an offering that he caught with his own divine hands . . . a present symbolic of his love for us."

I remembered hearing that the Savior owned a fifty- or sixty-foot, oceangoing yacht on which he held parties and went fishing.

Anselm continued, "And tonight all of the brothers and sisters can eat of the fish."

I hope they cook it first.

The family continued up the stairs to the bedrooms and the dressing rooms, and the disciples scurried about completing preparations for the evening meal.

The Savior and his board of directors reappeared about an hour later. The head man had changed to a white brocade, floor-length robe. They went into the dining room. Only the women were allowed to serve the meal. I heard about it from Sally, who doesn't take kindly to second-rate treatment of females.

Between enraged sputters, she told me that the food had to be handed to the Blessed One with two hands. Using one hand was a sign of disrespect. After placing the food before him, the server had to take three steps backward before leaving the august presence.

After the meal and some sacred belching, we were all gathered together in a large room and allowed to listen to the Savior deliver some words of inspiration and warnings about the dirty tricks of Satan. He had a strong voice and knew how to use it to get the disciples to freak out.

When he was done, Anselm raised his arms and announced, "Brothers and sisters, it's been a hot day and you've all worked hard. The Savior is allowing you to cool off in his swimming pool."

This was going to be interesting. As far as I knew, nobody had brought bathing suits. Evidently, a mass skinny dip was about to take place.

Wrong.

Everybody jumped into the pool with their clothes on. Laughing like demented lemmings.

We got back to our sleeping quarters about two o'clock in the morning.

As we were entering the stables, I caught sight of Harold. He looked totally out of it. I put my arm around his shoulders and led him off to one side. Quietly I said, "The Prophet stinks."

He glared at me and shouted, "Blasphemy!"

Several men looked at us. I was scared. In a voice as normal as I could make it, I replied, "You're right, Brother Jedediah, we must fight Satan. We must get

76

some rest now . . . so that we can work for the Savior tomorrow. Please, brother."

I soothed him and led him to his sleeping stall. All the time being watched by the curious brothers. He was so bushed that he fell off to sleep immediately.

It was time to crash out.

CHAPTER 12

My sleep was not peaceful. In a dream, I found myself in strange places and being pursued by frightening beings. I was running and shaking with fear.
Satan was chasing me. His bloodred eyes were filled
with hate. The snakes that grew out of his head, instead of hair, were flicking their forked tongues at
me. His tail wrapped around my running legs and
tripped me. I was caught. The devil nailed me to a
post with red-hot nails. His evil mouth shrieked,
"All heretics must burn." He threw a flaming torch
at my feet.

I woke up. My blanket was soaked with sweat.

After a few minutes I calmed down. In going over
the dream, I realized that while I had been consciously resisting the relentless propaganda, my sub-
conscious mind had been gathering and storing up
the phantoms and images that were constantly fed to
us. The shock of hearing Harold's response had
turned the demons loose in my head when I let down
my guard while sleeping.

Now I could better understand what had happened
to Harold.

He never believed that his thinking process could
be choked off and replaced by conditioned responses.
Like Pavlov's dogs. And so, he had taken no mental
or emotional precautions.

I felt guilty. I should have watched him more carefully. Now I had to get him out.

I was awake before the reveille bugle blasted.
Weariness, worry, frustration and disgust were be-

ginning to cloud my thoughts with a fuzziness that was frightening. I was in danger of losing control.

We must leave today.

At breakfast, I sought out Harold. "Good morning, brother," I said, faking cheerfulness with difficulty.

Harold eyed me warily. "Good morning."

"That was quite an experience."

"What was?"

"Seeing the Savior."

Harold's eyes brightened. "The most wonderful day of my life."

"Yes, yes. It was a revelation . . . the world should be told."

"It will be."

"I was thinking that you and I should carry the message to the outside world."

The look on his face changed. It became one of distrust. "What do you mean?"

"I had a vision that commanded us to go to your parents and tell them that they were wrong about Janice . . . I mean Grace."

"Why did you say Janice?"

My fears were confirmed. Harold had fallen off the edge.

"Satan used my tongue . . . but I fought him off."

Harold didn't buy it. "I think you are a doubter," he declared. With that he turned and walked away. A few minutes later, I saw him talking to the leader of his fund-raising team. From their glances toward me, I knew that I was the object of their conversation. Harold was probably telling him about our purpose in entering the commune.

Fortunately, a few minutes later Anselm's voice ordered us into the vans.

Our first selling stop was a large shopping center. Caleb gave orders to fan out in several directions to hustle donations by offering bags of peanuts.

Sally was sent down a wide mall heading east. I was given a small lane at a right angle to hers. As

79

soon as Caleb disappeared into a store, I hurried after Sally. When I caught up to her, she was sitting on a bench eating peanuts. She offered me a bag of nuts and said, "Your donation will go to combat pregnancy in runaway octogenarians."

"No time for promiscuous octogenarians, it's time for us teenagenarians to beat feet and head for the real world."

"What happened?"

"Harold flipped out."

"Oh, no."

"Have you been able to get anywhere with Janice?"

"She refuses to listen . . . and tries to avoid me."

"Well, that's it. Let's cancel our membership in Howdy-Doodyville and get out of here."

I looked around and saw two kids, about twelve years old, walking toward us. They were dressed in cutoff blue jeans, dirty sneakers and sloppy T-shirts. I beckoned to them. They came over somewhat doubtfully.

"Do you kids like peanuts?" I asked.

"Yeah."

"Well, you just won the mall contest for the neatest kids in the parade."

"What parade?"

"Shut up and take the peanuts."

I handed one of the kids the cardboard carton full of bags of nuts that I was carrying. Sally handed hers to the other kid.

"Gee, thanks," said both contest winners.

We found a taxi cab stand at the end of the mall. "How much to take us to Dundeen?"

"Twenty bucks."

"Let's go."

About half an hour later, the cab dropped us off at the garage where we had parked the rented car. The cab driver inspected the fifty-dollar bill I handed him with suspicion but he accepted it and gave me the change.

I telephoned the Barbors to tell them that we were starting on our way to their home.

Mr. Barbor answered the phone. "Where have you been? We've been worried."

"At the Savior of the Children camp."

"I called there several times and they said that they never heard of you."

"I'm not surprised. Honesty is not a big thing with them."

"Are Janice and Harold with you?"

"No . . . I'm sorry. We'll tell you all about it when we see you."

"Oh . . . I'm not really surprised."

"We'll see you soon."

"One other thing. The Gleasons are here . . . and so is Tommy."

CHAPTER 13

Tommy was home? That was an unexpected development. Sally and I speculated about its meaning as we drove back. Did he leave the cult? If so, how and why? Or was he there to pick up his car to turn over to the group? Or just to visit his parents? Just visiting his parents was unlikely. That was forbidden unless he was accompanied by at least two hard-core members of the organization. Well, whatever the reason, we'd soon find out.

An hour later we pulled up in front of the Barbor home. They must have been watching for us because as we were parking the car the five of them came out to greet us. Mr. and Mrs. Barbor, Mr. and Mrs. Gleason and Tommy Barbor or Tobias, as the case may be. After some concerned greetings, we were escorted into the house.

Tommy's manner and appearance had changed since our last meeting and parting. His eyes were alert. There was a warmth in his greeting and an eagerness to talk. No longer was he the zombielike Tobias.

Before we could find out the reason for the change, Mr. and Mrs. Gleason bombarded us with questions about Janice and Harold.

As we told the story, Tommy kept saying, "Yes . . . yes . . . of course . . . that's the way they operate," etc.

When we had finished, he said, "There's no time to lose. The longer we wait, the harder it will be."

Mr. Barbor then told us about Tommy. "He's been deprogrammed."

"He's been what?"

"Deprogrammed."

Then I remembered reading about the process. It was based on the assumption that cult members are "programmed" or brainwashed like prisoners of war. Through sleep deprivation, sensory bombardment, lack of privacy, poor diet and the desire to be accepted by the group, the individual is stripped of his ability or desire to think or act independently or critically.

The exact method of deprogramming was a little vague to me. I also remembered that it was not always successful.

Mr. Barbor continued the story: "The day after the three of you left to find Janice, I received a phone call from Tommy. It was a strange call. He asked that I clean out his savings account and send the money to him. When I asked him why, he gave me some confused reason. But more disturbing than that was the way he spoke. Somebody was obviously standing near him and prompting him. He would repeat my questions, then wait for his instructions before he replied."

Tommy nodded in agreement.

"As you know," continued Mr. Barbor, "I was very worried about Tommy before I got the call. As we were talking, I determined to do something about his situation . . . something drastic. But I pretended to go along with his request. I told him that his mother and I would bring the money to him. His prompter allowed him to tell us where he was staying . . . a place called Ephesus."

Tommy looked at me and said, "That's where they sent me after I lost you . . . to help me fight Satan and to strengthen my faith. Actually, it was a sort of punishment."

"After the call, I contacted a fellow who had

worked with cult members and had had success in bringing them out," said Mr. Barbor.

"They do the devil's work," said Tommy with a smile.

"The only problem was that he would talk to Tommy only if I brought Tommy to him. I could do this by getting a lawyer and going to court and obtaining a temporary conservatorship. Which means that I would have legal custody of Tommy for a short period of time. The legal process would take time and money and there was a chance that the court would deny the petition."

"The Savior has some high-priced lawyers doing his legal work for him and they know all the gimmicks to block this," said Tommy.

"So as far as I could see, the only thing left for me to do was to physically snatch Tommy and bring him to the deprogrammer."

Sally looked at Tommy's six-foot, two-hundred-pound frame and shook her head. "It's not like snatching a Barbie doll. Old Tommy could break a few noses if he decided to be unfriendly," she observed.

"It was worse than that," continued Mr. Barbor. "*I* could be thrown in jail for kidnapping . . . but I was so angry and upset that I didn't give a damn. I just could not conceive of anybody rescuing a prisoner of war and then being accused of kidnapping."

Mr. Gleason, who was listening with rapt attention, nodded his head in vigorous agreement.

"Damn right!" he exploded.

This sounded out of character for Mr. Gleason, who was a mild-looking man with horn-rimmed glasses and balding gray hair. He was short and thin and looked like the stereotype of a bookkeeper. Actually, he was an engineer.

"Talk about prisoner of war," interrupted Tommy. "Let me tell you about one thing that happened at Ephesus that will blow your minds."

We looked at Tommy.

"I was almost electrocuted," he said.

The looks turned to disbelief.

"Some kind of accident?" asked Mrs. Gleason, a stocky woman with a no-nonsense manner about her.

"No accident . . . it was one of the ways we proved our faith."

"Proved your faith?" exclaimed Mr. and Mrs. Gleason in unison.

"Yes. Those who were having their faith tested sat around in a circle holding hands. Except for two of the group who each held only one hand. With their other hand, they grabbed a small metal tube that was wired to a gadget connected to an electric outlet. When the gadget was turned on, an electric current ran through everybody holding hands in the circle. When a person dropped out, the circle got smaller and the current increased. You proved your faith by not dropping out. Well, it got down to two of us and the current got so strong that I thought I was going to die. I tried to let go of the other guy's hand but I was paralyzed. I could see that the same thing had happened to him. Somebody had a flash of sanity and yanked out the wall plug."

We all heard but scarcely believed our ears. Mr. Gleason was furious.

"I'd like to jam the Savior's nose into a wall socket and watch his eyeballs glow," he said.

Tommy's memories bubbled up as he continued. "Some of the girls were sent to Ephesus because they got pregnant; they stayed there until after the baby was born."

"I didn't think that wives were allowed to sleep with their husbands," said Mrs. Gleason.

"They're not. The girls who became pregnant had undergone some phony anti-Satan ritual with the cult leaders or even the Savior," replied Tommy.

By this time Mr. Gleason was livid. He was thinking of his daughter.

"If anybody touched Janice, I'll cut off his holy nose with a machete!" he exploded.

"But the worst of all," continued Tommy, "was that if a child cried, it was locked in a small dark closet until it stopped crying. And sometimes they forgot that the child was in the closet."

Everybody was appalled. Nobody spoke.

After a few seconds, Mr. Barbor continued the story of Tommy's rescue: "I called my brother, Ted, and he volunteered to help us. The three of us drove to Ephesus. When we got there, we lured Tommy out to the car by telling him that his mother was not feeling well and couldn't get out of the car. It was a hot day and we offered Tommy and his bodyguard a cool drink of orangeade. A drink that we had spiked with some knockout drops."

"I didn't approve of that," said Mrs. Barbor.

"If we hadn't done that, Tommy would still be plugged into the wall like a bed lamp," Mr. Barbor reminded her.

"Dad's right," said Tommy.

"We shoved Tommy into the car and drove to a motel and let him sleep off the drug. Then we called the deprogrammer," said Mr. Barbor.

"When I woke up in the strange bed, I knew that my parents were in league with Satan and I was going to be tortured. But I vowed to resist, no matter how much pain they inflicted on me. My faith would carry me through. We had been warned about the cruel, satanic deprogrammers," said Tommy.

"At first, Tommy kept chanting and refused to listen. But the sight of a beautiful shrimp cocktail and a juicy sirloin steak with fresh corn on the cob weakened his resistance," said Mr. Barbor.

"I agreed to discuss my faith with them. I was sure that I could convince them and even convert them," said Tommy.

"The thing that Tommy didn't know was that the deprogrammer had been a member of the cult for two years and knew more about it than Tommy. For two days, he quietly and persistently discussed its contradictions, its phony doctrines and the fact that its only purpose was to provide money-making slaves for the Savior by manipulating the idealism of young people," said Mr. Barbor.

"And Mom brought in some great home-cooked meals," said Tommy, laughing.

"Of course, the whole process is not quite as simple as I'm making it sound. It's not just a dose of love, reason and Mom's apple pie. Tommy had to be forced to explain and justify the lies, deceit and sexism used, condoned and taught by the cult. He had to think and not just act. And to understand that his feelings of compassion and yearnings for a larger truth are still part of himself," explained Mr. Barbor.

Tommy listened intently and his expression became very serious. "I would still like to become involved in religious work and find some meaning to existence," said Tommy.

"Your mother and I will be here to do what we can, even if it is only to listen," replied Mr. Barbor.

We were all silent for a while.

Mr. Gleason broke the silence. "Janice and Harold must have the same chance," he said.

"Right. Our immediate problem is to get them out of the cult. Any ideas?" asked Mr. Barbor.

CHAPTER 14

"Since Grant and I kissed them good-bye, there's very little chance of our getting back into the sanctuary," observed Sally.

"Their normal paranoia must be cranked up to a fever pitch since my disappearance," said Tommy.

"Going to any of their camp locations is completely ruled out. We have to pick up Janice and Harold while they are out fund-raising," said Mr. Barbor.

"How do we do that when we don't know where they are or where they'll be?" I asked.

We looked at each other. It seemed like our rescue mission was finished before it started.

"I've got an idea," said Sally.

"Yes?"

"We know the types of places they solicit. Suppose we split up into three teams, each team going in a different direction within a fifty-mile radius of Anselm's headquarters. As we go, we can ask the natives if any of the teams have been there. With persistence and a little luck we ought to be able to track them down."

It sounded reasonable.

"The basic idea is excellent. With a little refinement, I think it will work," I said. "We will need a control center and somebody to man it. The center will be this house and Mrs. Barbor and Mrs. Gleason will remain here. Each team will report, by telephone, every hour to the control center. If they spot the team we are looking for, the control center will be contacted immediately. When the other two teams phone in, they will be dispatched to the location to help pick up Janice and Harold."

Tommy had some cautionary words. "It may not be easy to get either of them away from the other cult members. There's liable to be a lot of screaming and resistance. It could get hairy."

"We'll do everything possible to avoid that, but since we don't know when or where we'll find them, I'm afraid we'll have to improvise when the time comes," I replied.

While the plan was far from perfect, it seemed like the only one possible, and after some discussion everybody agreed that we had to give it a try.

It was also decided that the only ones to do the actual snatching would be Mr. Gleason and Mr. Barbor. The search teams would be Sally and me in the rented car, Tommy and Mr. Gleason in Tommy's car, and Mr. Barbor and his brother, Ted, in the third car.

We got three sets of road maps and laid out a route for each team. Early the next morning, the three cars started on their assigned routes.

Sally and I stopped at any and all likely-looking places along our route but came up with only blank stares, or worse, to our questions. A somewhat typical encounter went like this:

I stopped a middle-aged man and asked him, "Did you see any young people asking for donations around here today?"

"I'm sorry, I'm not interested."

"No, no . . . I'm not selling anything."

"You want a donation? What for?"

"I don't want a donation. I'd like to know if you saw anybody asking for a charitable donation."

"What's he look like?"

"Who?"

"The fellow you're looking for."

"I hope I haven't bothered you, sir."

"No, no. That's all right. I'm always glad to help."

About three o'clock in the afternoon, we spotted one of the fund-raising vans in the parking lot of a small shopping center. We stayed out of sight and watched the van until the sales crew returned. Neither Janice nor Harold were part of the team.

From our hourly calls to the Barbor home we learned that two other vans had been sighted. But no sign of Harold or Janice.

The day passed without any further sightings of the Savior's sales force.

At dinner that night, we compared notes and felt that we were making progress and that the plan would succeed.

The next day Sally and I set out on a new route. Early in the day we got what seemed like a lucky break. Near a suburban bus terminal we saw Caleb's van. I knew it was Caleb's because I remembered a rusted gash in the right front fender. I parked where we could see the van but not too close to it. We slouched down in our seats to wait and watch. About ten minutes after parking, I saw Caleb walking toward the van. He was followed by Prudence. Then two other women and one man I vaguely recognized joined Caleb. No sign of Janice.

After the excitement of seeing Caleb's vehicle, not finding Janice was a tremendous letdown. We assumed that she was assigned to another leader. We spent the rest of the day in a fruitless search.

That evening, we learned that four more vans were found. None carried either Harold or Janice.

Tommy was depressed. He kept pulling his lower lip in gloomy thought. "We're not going to find either one of them in any of the vans," he said.

"Why do you say that?"

"I should have realized it before. First I was kidnapped, then Sally and Grant left . . . we're all connected to Janice and Harold. Now Anselm expects some action to remove Janice and Harold. I'm sure that he's hiding them somewhere. We'll never get them out."

"What are you talking about?" asked Mr. Gleason anxiously.

"They go absolutely crazy when somebody tries to defect . . . or parents make any moves to get their children out."

"What do they do?"

"I've heard of instances where they've sent kids to Canada or Mexico to avoid their being grabbed by their parents."

"Oh, no!" groaned Mr. Gleason.

"Lately, the Savior has employed legal counterattacks."

"Counterattacks?"

"Yes. He gets his high-priced lawyers to bring suits of kidnapping and attempted kidnapping against the parents."

I became more depressed.

"They're gone," asserted Tommy with gloomy finality.

"Not as long as I breathe," said Mr. Gleason.

I felt sick . . . and angry. There seemed to be no hope. I looked around. The sight of the depressed and distraught parents gave me an idea.

"There *is* something we can do," I said.

"What?"

"We can give them an opportunity to catch a parent in the act of kidnapping. I'm sure they'd like that. It would be a lesson to other meddlesome parents."

"I don't know exactly what you mean but it sounds dangerous," said Mrs. Gleason.

"I don't care how dangerous it is. Our children's lives are worth the risk," replied Mr. Gleason.

I outlined the plan. It was a long shot with a chance of success—if nothing unforeseen happened.

CHAPTER 15

I explained and refined the plan during the next hour. It was obvious that we couldn't rescue both Janice and Harold at the same time. The decision was to bring Janice out first.

The plan would be put into effect the next morning.

The first move was for Tommy to telephone Anselm at Bethel, where we had left Janice and Harold. The call was made from an outside booth. Tommy spoke in a low, hurried voice. "Hello, is this Prophet Anselm?"

"Yes."

"This is brother Tobias."

"Who?"

"Brother Tobias. I was at Ephesus. I was kidnapped."

"Oh, yes. I know about that. Where are you now?"

"I'm in a booth near my false parents' home . . . I slipped out for a minute. They've been working with Satan to break my faith . . . but I fooled them. When they talk, I think of the Savior."

"Good. Get away from there immediately . . . take a bus, taxi or anything. Then call me and tell me where you are and I'll send somebody to pick you up."

"Bless you, Prophet . . . but there is something else I have to tell you."

"What?"

"They're plotting to kidnap Sister Grace."

"Sister Grace? Oh, yes. Don't worry, they won't find her."

"Of course. With the Savior on our side, the forces of Satan will fail."

"Yes . . . now get out of there."

"First, I'd like my false parents punished. They must be taught a lesson . . . so that they'll leave us alone."

"What do you mean?"

"I have faith that you can devise a plan to trap them . . . to catch them in the act of kidnapping. It would serve them right."

"That's an interesting idea, Brother Tobias."

Anselm's ego was tickled and, also, this could be a way to make points with the Savior. Dragging parents into court with an open-and-shut case of kidnapping would put fear into the hearts of other scheming parents.

"Let me think about it. Can you call me back in an hour?" asked Anselm.

"Yes."

"Meantime go back and act natural."

"Bless you, Prophet."

Tommy seemed to relish the role of double agent. His performance was flawless.

An hour later Tommy called Anselm, who said, "Brother Tobias, your idea has merit. We have worked out a plan that will get the desired results."

"What is it?"

"All that I can tell you is that your false parents will get a call. It's better that you don't know any more. Have faith."

Evidently Anselm was taking no chances.

"Keep your thoughts on the Savior while you're near the servants of Satan," advised Anselm.

"Never fear, Prophet."

Back at the Barbor home, we waited anxiously for the promised call. When the phone rang we all jumped a little. Mr. Barbor picked it up.

"Hello."

"I'd like to speak to Mr. Alan Barbor."

"Speaking."

"Sir, my name is Johnson. I'm connected with the church, the Children of the Savior. We have reason to believe that your son plans to leave the church."

"Possibly."

"That is fine with us as long as it is of his own free will."

"I wouldn't have it any other way," said Mr. Barbor.

"You understand that all of our disciples are here by their own choice and conviction."

"To be bluntly honest, Mr. Johnson, I've had some doubts in the past."

"Ah, yes. We'd like to put your doubts to rest."

"How do you propose to do that?"

"Your niece is a member of our church and—"

"Wait, Mr. Johnson. My niece's father and mother are here now. Let me put Janice's father on the phone."

Mr. Gleason took the telephone from Mr. Barbor.

"Hello, this is Arthur Gleason."

"Yes, sir, nice to talk to you. As I was telling Mr. Barbor, your daughter, Sister Grace—"

"Janice."

"Ah, yes. Janice is a devoted and happy member of our organization."

"Devoted? Happy?"

"You seem to doubt me."

"I do."

"Would you like to meet her and see this for yourself?"

"Of course."

"Fine. She'll be with a few of her friends doing church work tomorrow in the Merit Mall, which, I believe, is about a forty-minute drive from where you now are. You can meet her and talk to her and convince yourself that she is happy and doing the work that is important to her."

"Tomorrow. At what time?"

"About noon . . . at the north end."

"Mrs. Gleason and I will be there."

"It was pleasant chatting with you."

So far the plan was working. Anselm was going to produce Janice for us. He was setting a trap.

Tommy made one more call to the sanctimonious spider who thought he was spinning a neat web to catch some juicy flies.

"Prophet Anselm, I can hardly wait to witness the divine punishment. My false father and false uncle are scheming to kidnap Sister Grace tomorrow."

"Don't worry, brother, we will be fully prepared."

"Good. Should I come with them?"

"Yes. After it's over, you can come home with us."

"Thank you, Prophet."

I doubt if any of us got much sleep that night.

CHAPTER 16

Early the next morning we were headed for the Merit Mall in three cars. The "snatch team" of Mr. Gleason and Mr. Barbor drove in the rented car. Ted Barbor, Mrs. Gleason and Mrs. Barbor were in Mr. Ted Barbor's car. Sally, Tommy and I followed behind in Tommy's car.

Before starting, Mr. Barbor had reserved two rooms in a motel about twenty minutes away from the Merit Mall.

We arrived at the mall at nine thirty, just as the doors were being opened. It was a small enclosed shopping mall with the main promenade running north and south. Two corridors came off at right angles to the wide walkway at about halfway down its length. The south end of the mall led into a department store. The north end, where Anselm was to produce Janice, had the usual cluster of chain, variety and fast-food stores.

I quickly surveyed the layouts of the stores at that end.

The one that best suited the rescue plan was a large shoe store. The entrance to the store, on the mall side, was the full width of the store. Another entrance was located at the other end of the store and opened onto the parking lot.

Perfect, I thought.

I walked through the center aisle of the store and out to the parking lot, then went to the rented car and drove it to a parking space about fifty feet from the door from which I had just exited. The car was positioned so that it could be driven directly out with no need to back up. Ready for a fast getaway. If everything went according to plan.

It was now ten o'clock. Time for a rehearsal. I reviewed the overall plan. Detailed movements could not be precisely anticipated since we didn't know our opponents' strategy. Most of our actions would have to be improvised.

We rehearsed the parts that put the plan into motion, then ran through possible courses that might follow. At eleven o'clock we took our assigned positions to wait for Anselm and his troops.

Sally, Tommy and I went into a fast-food shop on the side opposite the shoe store, about one hundred and fifty feet to the south of it. Mr. Barbor and Mr. Gleason went into a bookstore next to the shoe store, on the north side. The two wives went into a dress shop about halfway down the mall. Ted Barbor was leaning against the rented car, looking through the shoe store.

Sally, Tommy and I slowly sipped cups of coffee as we stood and watched the people strolling in the mall. Mr. Barbor and Mr. Gleason appeared to be browsing through books near the front of the bookstore. The two mothers were looking through racks of dresses.

Twelve o'clock came and went. No Janice and no Anselm.

At about ten after twelve, Tommy touched my arm and said, "There's one of the Savior's Swords," pointing to a muscular-looking young man in a white T-shirt, white slacks and white shoes who had just come through the north entrance to the mall.

"What's a Savior Sword?" I asked quietly.

"A member of the elite group that guards the Savior. Mean dudes," he replied.

Two more muscle men in white followed the first through the door. They paused, surveyed the area, then walked slowly down the esplanade, scrutinizing the people as they went.

We put down our coffee cups. I began to shake a little.

Then I saw her! Janice came through the door. Anselm was with her, his arm around her shoulders.

"This is it," I said.

Just then two cops came in.

"Oh, no. What do we do now?" asked Tommy.

"We'll debate about it later. Right now, it's full speed ahead and damn the torpedoes," answered Sally.

"Let's go!" I said.

Sally and I ran out of the coffee shop and headed south, away from Janice and Anselm. Tommy followed us. When we had gone one hundred feet, Sally and I stopped. I put my arms around Sally's waist and lifted her off the ground. As I did this, Tommy let out a yell, "Kidnapping! Kidnapping! Kidnapping!" as he pointed to me holding Sally.

Then he ran down the aisle, took a right turn into one of the side corridors and disappeared through a mall exit.

The commotion was something to see. As the Savior's goons and the two cops rushed up to us, Sally and I put our lips together in an Oscar-winning kiss. And held it.

"What's going on here?" demanded one of the cops.

I put Sally down. Slowly. We both smiled.

"He just popped the question," Sally told the cop.

"What question?"

"Oh, you know, silly goose. Would I marry him," replied Sally.

"What was the yelling about?"

"Oh, that was Ralph. He's very emotional. He thinks Grant stole me from him. He's really a dear, and he'll get over it."

Out of the corner of my eye, I could see some of the

action back where Janice and Anselm had been. A second after Tommy let out his scream, Mr. Barbor and Mr. Gleason ran out of the bookstore toward Janice and Anselm. Mr. Barbor pushed Anselm aside while Mr. Gleason put his arm around his daughter's waist and hustled her into the shoe store and out the back door. Ted Barbor was in the driver's seat with the motor running. Mr. Gleason pushed Janice into the back of the car and followed her in. Disengaging himself from Anselm, Mr. Barbor then sprinted through the shoe store and jumped into the front seat with Ted. The car roared off.

Meantime, back at our charade, things were getting weird. Anselm came pounding up, yelping, "She's been kidnapped, she's been kidnapped."

When he saw Sally and me, he recognized us and became hysterical. Pointing to us, he shouted, "They're part of the plot."

Sally looked at him and said, "Please, sir, get hold of yourself. We'll get our parents' permission. Until then we'll only hold hands."

Anselm's eyes began to bug out. "Arrest them! Arrest them!" he bellowed.

"For what?" inquired a cop.

"Kidnapping."

Just then Mrs. Gleason and Mrs. Barbor joined the excitement. Mrs. Gleason pointed to Anselm and asked, "Are you Prophet Anselm?"

Anselm looked surprised, then replied, "Yes."

Mrs. Gleason turned to the police and said, "Officers, I want that man arrested for fraud, deceit, illegal detention *and* kidnapping."

"What?"

"He kept my daughter, Janice, captive, violating her constitutional rights."

The cops sensed that this was getting beyond their scope of authority. They were looking for a way to get away gracefully. The older of the two turned to the other and said, "This seems to be a family disagreement. There are no grounds to make an arrest."

Anselm was having none of this.

"Sister Grace has been abducted."

"Who?"

"The girl I brought here."

Sally looked at Anselm. "Oh no, sir. I saw the girl that was with you walk away by herself when you came running down here."

"That was my daughter," said Mrs. Gleason.

The cops were way out of their depth. The older policeman said, "Sir . . . madam . . . I suggest that you each get legal counsel to resolve your differences."

With that, the cops walked away with all the official dignity they could muster.

People were milling around trying to figure out what was happening.

Anselm's troops clustered around him waiting for orders. Sally walked over to him and with a sweet smile said, "Sir, I heard you say that you are a prophet. Would you be kind enough to favor us with a prophecy? Something we could cherish."

Anselm was livid. "You have not heard the end of this," he muttered.

"I was hoping for something more spiritual," replied Sally.

By now, Mrs. Gleason and Mrs. Barbor had disappeared. It was time for Sally and me to leave the scene.

I raised my hand and gave a friendly wave to Anselm.

"Bless you," I said.

CHAPTER 17

Janice and her mother stayed at the motel for three days. A psychologist with extensive experience with cult methods counseled them. Janice had plenty of rest, good food and lots of understanding, patience and real love from her parents.

They told her that if she still wanted to return to the cult after listening to and discussing the contradictions between what the sect professed and what it actually did, they would not stand in her way.

On the morning of the third day, Janice hugged her parents. Everybody cried.

They tell me that it will not be easy for Janice to find her true self. I suspect that she will keep seeking answers for many years to come.

In the euphoria that followed Janice's rescue, Harold's situation was blotted from our minds. But only briefly.

Snatching Harold from the cult was going to be much more difficult as a result of the sect's loss of Janice and Tommy. Their normal paranoia would be increased to hysteria, and any actions against them could be dangerous. However, whatever the risk, we were determined to attempt a rescue.

For several days we discussed and explored the possibilities. No plan with a reasonable or even slight chance of success could be found.

Then one morning the local newspaper had a small article about a mass wedding ceremony to be performed by the Savior of the Children.

Janice read it, smiled and said, "I guess they'll

have to get another wife for old what's-his-name now."

I remembered that Janice had been scheduled to marry a Savior-chosen husband. A man unknown to her. Janice handed the paper to Sally. She read the piece carefully.

"The wholesale wedding is scheduled for two weeks from now. That may be our chance," she said.

"Chance for what?" I asked.

Sally regarded me with the patient look of a mother about to explain something to her dear but slow-witted offspring.

"To pull Harold out of the cult."

"Oh . . . of course. I was just checking to see if you realized it. What are you talking about?"

"The mass wedding could be the perfect cover for us to penetrate the cult, find Harold and get him out," explained Sally.

"You mean we could pose as one of the prospective wedding couples and crash the party?"

"Right on, my dear Watson."

"Right on, my foot. There are more flaws in that idea than there are seeds in a pumpkin. But I like it. We'll work on the flaws later."

"I thought you would." Sally turned to Janice. "Is there any chance that Harold will be one of those chosen to be married?"

"I'm almost certain that he will be. You see, they intend to marry all members who are not already married," replied Janice.

"Why's that?"

"Once they are married, it will make it more difficult for the parents to pull them out of the group, it will tie them closer to the Savior. It might be impossible if they become pregnant."

"Are they planning a mass impregnation? I'd like to get tickets to that," I said.

Sally looked at me in disgust.

"Only to further my research into mass sociological phenomena," I explained.

"What happens if they have less men than women or vice versa?" asked Sally.

"I don't know but I'm sure they'll give priority to those who may be vulnerable to parental pressure to leave the sect."

The newspaper article reported that about ninety couples were to be wed. The ceremony was to be held in a nearby indoor sports arena.

It occurred to me that the Children of the Savior would not even come close to getting into the Guiness's book of records, when it came to mass weddings. The Moonies had married two thousand and seventy-five couples in Madison Square Garden in New York. Couples that had not even had a chance to *watch* "The Dating Game," much less play it.

Looking through the sports section of the newspaper, I saw that a basketball game was scheduled to be played at the arena the following night. Sally and I decided to attend the game and scout the layout of the arena and the surrounding area.

It was a thirty-minute drive from the Barbor home to the stadium. The building had one main entrance and eight exit doors and was surrounded by a large paved parking lot. The exit doors were kept locked and could only be opened from the inside with panic bars. The entrance gate was manned by ticket takers and private security guards.

We were certain that on the day of the wedding the security provided by the cult would be heavy. Getting into the festivities would be difficult if not impossible. The obvious way around the problem would be to grab Harold before he entered the arena.

One other possibility occurred to me.

"Why don't we come in the night before, attend whatever event takes place, then hide somewhere in the building after it's over and spend the night inside the arena. We could bring food in with us."

Sally looked skeptical but said, "It might have a chance. Let's check to see what's playing."

We found one of the ushers and asked him what game was scheduled for the fifteenth of the month, the day before the wedding. He took a schedule out of his pocket, consulted it and said, "Nothing on the calendar for the fourteenth or the fifteenth."

Unless we set up housekeeping in the auditorium, an early entry was out.

There was no doubt about it. We had to rescue Harold before he entered the wedding pit. Only careful planning would give us a reasonable chance of success.

During the ride back to the Barbor home we started working on the details.

CHAPTER 18

The best way for us to get close enough to Harold to be able to abduct him would be for us to mingle with the prospective brides and grooms as they arrived at the stadium. We had no way of knowing when and by what means they would come. According to the news release, the wedding was to take place at noon. So we planned on being there by eight o'clock in the morning. Dressed as a bride and groom.

This was going to present a problem. We would look suspicious hanging around the entrance. Somebody was sure to question us and there was no plausible way we could explain our presence there.

The other difficulty was that we would need a vehicle parked close by into which I could hustle Harold when the time came.

Both problems were solved by the same device.

We would rent a van or panel truck. On each side of the van we would tape a sign that read FIRST AID SERVICE. The signs would not be put on until we were close to the arena. Mr. Gleason would drive the van wearing a white jacket similar to those worn by ambulance drivers. On the seat next to him would be a large first-aid kit. He would park the vehicle close to the arena entrance. Too conspicuous to arouse suspicion.

Sally and I would stay hidden in the van until we could safely mingle with the arriving wedding couples.

We kept the plan as simple as possible. The more

complications we introduced, the more chances there would be for a foul-up.

When we spotted Harold, whose cult name I remembered as Jedediah, Sally would set up a diversionary action to draw attention away from me as I approached him. She would start yelling about Satan, rape or the dangers of sugar in the diet. Whatever seemed appropriate.

While Sally was giving her performance, I would quickly get to Harold and briskly escort him to the van. I didn't see this as any problem since I'm at least fifty pounds heavier than he is and Harold's life as a would-be accountant hadn't done much for his muscular development. In an emergency, I could tell him that I was from the IRS and we needed him to conduct an audit of his income-tax return. He might not fully believe this but it would keep him occupied until I stuffed him into the van.

Naturally, I would be disguised. My blond hair would be dark, a pair of horn-rimmed glasses would give me a scholarly look and I would grow or glue on a mustache. Sally said that I shouldn't count on growing one in time.

We checked the plan with the Barbors and the Gleasons. They agreed that only three of us should be involved, Mr. Gleason, Sally and me. More than that would attract attention, and the success of the plan depended on speed and surprise, not numbers.

Sally arranged to rent a simple wedding dress, white shoes and a veil. Tommy would lend me a blue suit, white shirt and a tie.

The only thing left to do was to get the signs painted for the van and to rent the van.

Near the Barbor home was a truck and recreational-vehicle renting firm. Mr. Gleason, Sally and I drove there to make the arrangements. We found a panel truck that suited our purpose, signed a contract and left a deposit. As we were leaving, Sally turned to me and asked, "How would you like to play house?"

I stopped. Not sure that I had heard what I thought I heard.

"What? Did you say 'play house'?"

"Yes."

I looked at this beautiful creature who could turn me into a pillar of salt, whose lips could caress me into a quivering mass of jello, and I could not believe my incredible luck.

"You mean . . . ?"

"No."

"Oh."

She laughed.

"I mean cooking and cleaning and taking out the garbage and if you play your cards right, I'll nag you occasionally."

"Careful. You're talking major commitment and love beyond reason," I said as I tried to figure out what she was talking about.

Sally pointed to small Winnebago motor homes parked in the rental company's lot. The kind that have cooking facilities, an eating area, sleeping bunks, a shower, storage cabinets, etc.

"Let's rent one of those for a week and take a vacation cruising the California coast. I'll drive and you can cook. Harold's rescue attempt is ten days away and there's nothing more we can do around here until then."

It sounded beautiful.

"I don't dust, vacuum or do windows," I said.

"We'll have a maid come in once a week."

We hurried back to the salesman. Who promptly punctured the dream.

"I'm sorry. I can't rent a vehicle to you. You have to be twenty-five."

It looked like we were done in again by the Denture-Grip crowd.

Back at the Barbor home Tommy asked why we

were so glum. When we told him, he said, "Take my car and camping equipment. You may never get another chance to see the California coast."

Before the sun was up the next morning, we were on our way to check out what Balboa had discovered.

CHAPTER 19

The week that followed should be engraved by an angel in Abou ben Adam's book of gold.

If I live to be one hundred and six, I doubt if I will ever be happier than I was during those days with Sally.

The world of ever-present problems and meanness ceased to exist. There was only the beauty that surrounds us waiting to be discovered; unspoken love waiting to be expressed; senses, dulled by the everyday burdens of living, waiting to spring to life. All waiting.

We found them, expressed them and felt them.

We saw the wondrous shapes and colors of the landscape, we heard the roar of the ocean, the murmur of brooks and the songs of the birds, we smelled the fragrances of glorious blooms . . . all through one set of senses. It was as if we shared the same eyes and ears.

And, at times, one body.

We found a secluded beach on which we felt as remote from other humans as Robinson Crusoe on his island.

We swam in the gentle Pacific, then sat on blankets on the warm sand holding each other as we watched the glowing red sun ease itself into the water.

Holding each other silently was like the quiet soaring of birds through a caressing cloud. We floated on warm updrafts, then swiftly glided down in breathtaking sweeps of excitement. The caressing cloud enveloped us again and we drifted weightless through the soft glow of an unseen light.

* * *

Only once during the week did we think of the problem that lay ahead of us. As we drove past the railroad station of a small town, we saw a group of Hari Krishna adherents in their saffron robes, chanting and doing their rhythmic and mystic stomp.

The sight set off a train of thought about Harold in each of us. I soon put it out of my mind. Sally must have had more difficulty doing this. After our evening meal on a beach, Sally was writing postcards to friends and family. She started to write one to the Gleasons and Barbors to tell them that we were enjoying ourselves, etc. when she looked up and said, "At least he doesn't have to shave his head and clang those finger bells."

"What?"

"Harold . . . maybe we should be thankful that the Krishnas didn't get him."

"Oh."

"If only we could get into the arena . . . it might give us more time and opportunity."

"Forget it. There's no way. There'll be guards at the door and probably everybody will have a special pass or ticket."

With that Sally became silent. A little while later she handed me a postcard. It was one of the kind that you buy at the post office. Blank on both sides except for the printed postage mark in one corner. On the empty side she had neatly lettered with a thin, felt-tip marking pen:

```
┌─────────────────────────────────┐
│                                 │
│     SPECIAL ENTRY PERMIT        │
│                                 │
│      HONORED COUPLE             │
│                                 │
│     RESERVED SECTION            │
│                                 │
└─────────────────────────────────┘
```

In the corners she had drawn little flowers and hearts.

"There's our ticket," she said.

I looked at it and laughed. "We'd have a better chance with a 'CHICKEN INSPECTOR' badge." I kissed her and said, "Please forget it. We're on vacation . . . and it's not helping Harold."

"You're right . . . and I will."

We didn't think about it again until we returned to the Barbor home.

CHAPTER 20

The tension at the Barbor house was high and mounting. The mass wedding had received more publicity and Mr. Gleason was afraid that a large number of curiosity seekers would make our task more difficult. In addition to the sect's security precautions there was sure to be a contingent of local police.

The rescue attempt was to be made the next day. Mr. Gleason had picked up the van and the signs. He made arrangements for the deprogrammer to be available and reserved a place to bring Harold for counseling after the rescue.

The wedding dress was ready for Sally. I darkened my hair and bought a false mustache in a place that rented costumes for theatrical productions. They also had a pair of heavy horn-rimmed spectacles with plain glass that gave me that mild-mannered Clark Kent look. Except that under my conservative blue suit was no Superman underwear.

We were up at five o'clock. By dawn we saw that the day would be overcast and there was a threat of rain in the air. That was one problem that we hadn't anticipated. If it rained heavily, the couples would probably run to the entrance, thereby reducing the time available for us to act, and Sally's diversion would lose its impact. There was nothing we could do to change the weather except do a short sun dance before we headed for the festivities.

Sally looked beautiful in the white, lace-trimmed, short wedding dress. The blond hair of the wig reached her shoulders in soft curls and the veil covered her blue eyes.

In an attempt to ease the tension, I said, "If we foul up and blow it—so it shouldn't be a total loss—why don't we drive to Nevada and have a quickie wedding of our own?"

The tension remained about the same.

Mr. Gleason donned a white medical-type jacket and a white ambulance-driver's cap and slid into the driver's seat of the dark blue van. Sally and I entered the rear of the van and sat on a cot that we had set up to give the first-aid vehicle a more authentic look. We had draped a dark blue curtain between the driver's section and the interior of the van. A large first-aid kit was on the seat next to Mr. Gleason. It was now seven o'clock.

Thirty minutes later we were about half a mile from the arena. Mr. Gleason pulled off the main road onto a side street and stopped the car. We unrolled the signs and taped them to the sides of the van.

Soon we were on our way to a mass-wedding-minus-one in a vehicle that would provide "FIRST AID SERVICE."

At least, that was what the sign stated. The sky was overcast but no rain yet.

Mr. Gleason parked the van about two hundred feet from the entrance. He assumed a bored expression and remained in the driver's seat while Sally and I stayed out of sight inside the van.

Nobody else was there.

At nine o'clock, employees of the arena arrived and entered the building. At ten o'clock, a squad of about fifteen local policemen drove up in a police van. There was a nervous moment when the sergeant in charge looked toward our van, waved and said, "Good idea. I hope you have plenty of aspirin."

Then he turned his attention to stationing his men at strategic points around the building. Soon the parking lot began to fill. Friends, relatives, curiosity

113

seekers and reporters headed for the entrance but were kept back temporarily by sawhorses set up by the police.

Marriage is supposed to be a happy occasion but there were very few smiles on the faces of the guests.

At about a quarter to eleven, five large buses entered the parking field, pulled up and parked in a single file, one behind the other. The first bus was about twenty feet from us.

Sally and I watched nervously through the small windows in the rear doors.

It was show time.

We were going to have to make some quick and correct decisions. Fortunately, the buses did not discharge their passengers all at the same time. They started to empty the buses one at a time, beginning with the first bus. I assumed that this was done to keep things more orderly and controlled.

The first ones out of the first bus were neither brides nor grooms but goons. Swords of the Savior, muscle men of the Children of the Savior. Dressed in tight-fitting, white T-shirts, white slacks and white shoes. About twenty of them marched up to the entrance in a column of twos. There they split into single lines on either side of the entrance, extending outward from the entrance and forming a gauntlet through which everyone entering the arena would have to pass. Anyone without proper credentials would have no chance of forcing his way in. This precaution was, no doubt, aimed at disgruntled parents who were not invited.

Then the first bridal couple came out of the first bus. It was time to make our move.

Knowing that it would look suspicious if we just stood around searching for Harold, we devised a reason for not walking toward the arena. Sally had marked the palm of her left hand with red ink so that it looked like she had cut herself and was bleeding. At a signal from me, Mr. Gleason would take the first-aid kit and step out of the van while we slipped out through the rear doors. Sally in her bridal gown and me in a blue suit and mustache. We would meet at the side of the van and Mr. Gleason would get busy dressing her apparent wound and bandaging her hand while Sally and I checked the approaching couples for a sign of Harold.

During the time that it took us to get out of the van and begin our little charade, six or seven couples had passed us and were walking between the lines formed by the Swords of the Savior.

I looked at the couples exiting the buses and coming toward us. No sign of Harold. Sally glanced at the backs of the couples just about to enter the bridal circus. I heard her groan, "Oh, no!"

"What?" I asked.

"It can't be."

I looked to where she was pointing.

"I think that's Harold," she said.

Mr. Gleason's head spun around and the three of us stared as the ticket taker extended his hand to a man that looked like Harold from the rear. The man handed something to the attendant and started to walk through the gate followed by his bride-to-be. We both looked at Mr. Gleason.

"That's Harold. I'm going after him," he said.

I grabbed his arm.

"No, it won't help . . . and you might get hurt."

"I don't care."

He was frantic.

I felt like I had walked off the end of a cliff. All that planning and those hopes going up in smoke because we looked away for two minutes.

Mr. Gleason tried to pull away from my grasp. Sally tried to calm him down.

Suddenly she left us, ran to the rear of the van and entered it. She was back in a minute holding the postcard she had lettered.

SPECIAL ENTRY PERMIT

HONORED COUPLE

RESERVED SECTION

"Let's try to crash with this," she said.

"Ridiculous!" I replied.

She looked at it and nodded her head.

"I know," she said, sounding very depressed.

We stood there in total frustration. Then an idea began to form in my numbed brain.

"Wait. The opera's not over till the fat lady sings," I said.

They looked at me as though the disappointment had unhinged my loosely anchored mind.

"Mr. Gleason, keep bandaging Sally's hand till I get back," I ordered.

Then I took the postcard from Sally and walked toward the couples gathered near the fourth bus. They were waiting for a signal to start toward the arena. I looked them over quickly and picked a likely-looking couple. He was short and thin and seemed ill at ease. His Savior-chosen bridal candidate was taller and heavier with the serene air of a pilgrim headed for Mecca.

I approached them in my best official manner. Putting my hand on his shoulder, I quietly asked, "You are Brother . . . ?"

He looked surprised but answered, "Micah."

"Right . . . and this, of course, is Sister . . . ?"

"Miriam," she replied.

"Thank God I found you in time. The Savior will be pleased."

"What?"

I placed my arm around his shoulders and led him

a short distance away from the other couples. Miriam followed.

"I have been sent by the Savior to seek you out."

They looked at me. Confused.

"As you know, the Savior sees into the hearts and minds of all those who serve him."

They nodded.

"This morning he called me into his presence and said, 'Seek out Brother Micah and Sister Miriam and tell them of my pleasure in their work and sacrifice.'"

They lowered their eyes in shy acknowledgment.

"And he has decided to reward you."

They looked up in surprise.

"You have been chosen to sit near him during the ceremony . . . in a section reserved for the most devout . . . in fact, I have the invitation and special pass written with his own sacred hand to give to you."

I briefly waved Sally's work in front of their bewildered faces.

"Do you have your entry pass to the ordinary seats?"

"Yes," replied Micah, showing me an embossed 3x5 card with some gold engraving on it.

"And yours, Sister Miriam?" I asked.

She wrinkled her brow in confusion.

"I have none. We were both told to use Brother Micah's."

"Of course, of course . . . the excitement of this glorious day has made me forgetful."

I eased the engraved card from Micah's fingers and extended Sally's card to him.

"Take this with the Savior's blessing."

He took it.

I lowered my voice and leaned toward them. "Now, brother and sister, listen carefully. Wait until the couples from the last bus have entered the arena. Then present yourselves. You will be escorted to the special section." I raised the palm of my right hand toward them. "Bless you both."

I hurried back to Sally and Mr. Gleason.

By this time, the couples from the second bus had entered and the third busload was starting to move.

Sally's left hand had a bandage wrapped around it and Mr. Gleason was examining it.

I took Sally's arm.

"Come on, we mustn't keep the preacher waiting." Turning to Mr. Gleason, I said, "Wait here with the engine running. We may have to leave suddenly."

Sally and I fell in with the slowly moving group from the third bus.

"What's the plan?" whispered Sally.

"As soon as I figure it out, I'll let you know."

"Great."

We walked through the gauntlet and I handed the engraved card to the man at the gate. He nodded as we went through. We were motioned to follow the couple in front of us.

A thought occurred to me. I leaned close to Sally and said, "Take off the bandage."

I realized that if Micah and Miriam raised a fuss, the security forces would be looking for a woman with a bandaged hand and a man with a dark mustache.

I bent over, covered the lower part of my face with my left hand and pulled the mustache off with my right. It brought tears to my eyes.

Sally looked at me and handed me the crumpled bandage. I shoved it into my jacket pocket.

Monitors were assembling the expectant couples in the lounge and refreshment area behind the main auditorium. Somebody with a bullhorn was saying, "Please remain quiet. We must wait for the guests to be seated before we begin the march down the aisle. Take note of the couple in front of you and when the hymn starts follow that couple . . . when we give the signal."

The couple behind us studied Sally and me. I pointed to the tears in my eyes and whispered, "I'm so happy, I'm crying."

They nodded sympathetically.

Harold was somewhere in front of us but we couldn't find him immediately. Then Sally spotted him. He was third from the head of the line.

"Any ideas yet?" she asked.

"I'm working on it."

"Well, stop working . . . it's time to get into gear. I'm going to get sick. Help me to the ladies room . . . move us to Harold."

With that she let out a low moan and leaned against me. I put my arm around her waist and said, "She's sick . . . oh, oh . . . excuse me, excuse me . . ."

While saying that, I began to push our way toward the front of the line.

"Excuse me, excuse me . . . she needs air . . . air."

The people opened the way for us. Between moans, Sally whispered, "Get Harold to help carry me out."

It was a great idea but how was I going to do that? We continued to move toward the head of the line.

"Pardon me . . . excuse us . . . she'll be all right as soon as she gets a little air . . . sorry."

When we were within two feet of Harold, Sally whispered, "Let go of me."

I did. She took two steps, let out a moan, collapsed with her back against Harold and started to slide to the floor. Harold instinctively caught her under her armpits. He seemed bewildered.

"Oh, thank you, brother," I said.

I bent down and picked up Sally's legs.

"Bless you for your help."

I began moving toward an exit and Harold followed. He had no choice unless he dropped Sally. The other couples looked concerned and cleared the way for us.

The exit was only a short distance away. I pushed the panic bar with my backside and the door opened.

"There is a first-aid ambulance just a short distance away. It's so kind of you to offer your help," I said as I pulled Sally and Harold along.

He looked at me strangely. My dark hair and horn-rimmed glasses made recognition difficult. The excitement and strain of carrying Sally didn't help.

There were no security guards stationed at the exit. Almost everybody had entered the arena by this time.

We were about one hundred feet away from our van when a Sword of the Savior approached us. Damn. All we needed now was to be stopped by a six-foot Unfriendly Creepy Object.

"What happened?" he asked.

"My bride fainted from the heat and excitement," I said as I kept walking.

He looked at Harold and said, "I'll help him, brother. You can return to the ceremony."

He moved close to Sally in order to relieve Harold of his burden. Sally increased her moaning and began to twitch and wave her arms.

When the Sword was almost directly above her, she swung her right arm up sharply. It flew upward between the white trousered legs of the Sword.

That must have smarted.

He doubled over in pain and surprise.

"She must be having an epileptic seizure," I said to Harold and the now kneeling Sword.

"Let's hurry to the ambulance . . . then we'll come back for this injured brother," I continued.

A minute later we were at the van. The back doors were open and Mr. Gleason was slouched down in the front seat with a cap pulled down hiding his face. The engine was running.

"Help me get her on the cot in the ambulance," I said to Harold, maneuvering so that he would have to enter first. He grunted and strained as he stepped up into the van and began pulling Sally in.

With all the jostling, Sally's wig became twisted and the curls fell in front of her face. As he set her down on the cot, the wig fell off and Harold stared at her. Shocked. I don't know whether it was because he recognized Sally or because he thought her hair falling out was an indication of something terminal.

A second later, he knew it was Sally. He screamed, "Kidnappers!" and started for the doors. I grabbed him, wrapped my arms around him and held on while he tried to drag me out of the van.

Mr. Gleason heard the bellow, jumped out of the driver's seat, ran to the rear, and slammed and locked the doors.

Five seconds later Sally, Harold and I were bouncing around inside the van as it gained speed and headed down the highway.

EPILOGUE

Strangely, Harold ceased all resistance and went limp as soon as the van doors shut. He sat on the cot in sort of a trance and kept repeating, "Satan, I will defeat you. My faith is strong."

It was almost as if he were trying to convince himself.

When we arrived at the motel rooms that Mr. Gleason had reserved, the psychologist-deprogrammer was waiting. He was a tall, gray-haired man with a kind and patient manner. He greeted Harold with warm friendliness.

"Hello, Harold. I'm sorry that we had to meet this way but I'm afraid there was no choice."

Harold looked off into the distance and said, "Satan, I will defeat you. My faith is strong."

"Good. I'd like to talk to you about faith . . . if you'll let me," replied Mr. Johnson, the deprogrammer.

During the next three days, Mr. and Mrs. Gleason occupied a room next to Harold's. Janice was with them during the day and spent the nights at the Barbors.

I think that Janice was the greatest influence in getting Harold to understand what had happened to him. He was able to relate to her and she could identify with him. They spoke for hours and she was able to get him to examine his experience with some objectivity.

On the third day, the breakthrough came with an unexpected suddenness.

"Mother and Dad must have gone through a terrible time," he said.

We all celebrated the reunion of the family at a local restaurant. With lots of food, laughter and more than a few tears.

The summer was over and Sally and I had to return home.

On the flight back, Sally turned to me and said, "I'm sure glad that we don't have to write any more of those high-school English compositions on 'How I Spent My Summer Vacation.'"

"You're right," I agreed. "What could we write about?"

M. ARTHUR BOGEN's career has had a wide range. After receiving his undergraduate degree with a major in psychology, he went on to get a degree in engineering. To fill in the time while he mastered typing, he passed the course for certification as a meteorologist and spent a few years as a weather officer in the Air Force.

His career as a practicing parent has been acknowledged to be an outstanding success by his two daughters or one of their envious friends. He forgets which. One daughter is a high school guidance counselor and the other is studying law. Any resemblance of his daughters to characters in his books is purely coincidental or quite deliberate according to his wife, a professional artist.

A BURCHARDT & DECKER MYSTERY
M. ARTHUR BOGEN

Meet super sleuths Grant Decker and Sally Burchardt in these Flare mysteries:

MIND GAMES 86512-2/$2.25
While vacationing in California after their high school graduation, Sally and Grant try to track down a missing girl. But when Grant finds himself forgetting things—he suddenly realizes that he and Sally are being brainwashed by a dangerous religious cult!

BARELY UNDERCOVER 85217-9/$2.25
When Grant hears about the arrest of Tommy Deland for typewriter theft, he can hardly believe his ears! Tommy wouldn't know what to do with a typewriter, never mind how to get rid of a hot one. Grant and Sally try to help their friend, but Grant has problems when the police suspect *him* of being a thief, so before they can prove Tommy's innocence, Sally has to get Grant out of trouble.

DOUBLE DEALING 83394-8/$2.25
When 17-year-old Grant is busted for the possession of ten pounds of marijuana found in his locker, he finds out that it was no student prank. Grant and Sally decide that they must find the true identity of the drug dealer to save Grant from prosecution!

NOVELS FROM AVON ◆ FLARE

CLASS PICTURES   61408-1/$1.95

Marilyn Sachs

Pat, always the popular one, and shy, plump Lolly have been
best friends since kindergarten, through thick and thin,
supporting each other during crises. But everything changes
when Lolly turns into a thin, pretty blonde and Pat finds
herself playing second fiddle for the first time.

THE GROUNDING OF GROUP 6   83386-7/$2.50

Julian Thompson

What do parents do when they realize that their sixteen-year
old son or daughter is a loser and an embarrassment to the
family? Five misfits find they've been set up to disappear at
exclusive Coldbrook School, but aren't about to allow themselves to be permanently "grounded".

JACOB HAVE I LOVED   62521-0/$2.25

Katherine Paterson

Do you feel that no one understands you? Louise's pretty twin
sister, Caroline, has always been the favored one, while Louise
is ignored and misunderstood. Now Louise feels that Caroline
has stolen from her all that she has ever wanted...until she
learns how to fight for love and the life she wants for herself.

TAKING TERRI MUELLER   79004-1/$2.25

Norma Fox Mazer

Was it possible to be kidnapped by your own father? Terri's
father has always told her that her mother died in a car
crash—but now Terri has reason to suspect differently, and
she struggles to find the truth on her own.

FRIENDS FOR LIFE   82578-3/$2.25

Ellen Emerson White

On the day pretty high school senior Susan McAllister begins
school at Beacon Hill, she finds that her best friend has
supposedly died of an overdose of drugs. But Susan is sure
it was murder and is determined to find the truth, despite
the danger of becoming another victim.